MAYHEM IN EUREKA COUNTY

A Terrence Corcoran Western

JOHNNY GUNN

WOLFPACK
PUBLISHING
— EST 2013 —

Mayhem in Eureka County
Paperback Edition
Copyright © 2022 Johnny Gunn

Wolfpack Publishing
5130 S. Fort Apache Rd. 215-380
Las Vegas, NV 89148

wolfpackpublishing.com

Paperback ISBN 978-1-63977-441-8
eBook ISBN 978-1-63977-440-1
LCCN 2022942801

MAYHEM IN EUREKA COUNTY

CHAPTER ONE

SPRING SEEMED to be on just about everyone's mind in the sprawling Nevada mining camp known as Eureka. Heavy winter snows were finally beginning to melt fast creating rushing streams, creeks, and rivers along with vast areas of mud. Eureka sat on a hillside at the southern end of the Diamond Range with the town's western flanks overlooking the southern Diamond Valley while its eastern flank was the Eureka Canyon.

"Preacher Ned is calling it a biblical flood, Terrence. I'd call it an early thaw." Ed Connor stood on the wooden planks of the sidewalk in front of the Eureka County Sheriff's Office, his tin sheriff's badge gleaming in the early spring sun, his ever-present tin coffee cup steaming away.

"When all this water makes its way up north to join the Humboldt River, old Ned might just be right." Terrence Corcoran was Ed Connor's chief deputy and best friend. The two had different ways of practicing the ancient art of keeping the peace but never let it affect their friendship.

Corcoran was tough, believed in the letter of the law, but had a compassionate side that allowed a man to make a mistake, but only once. Connor on the other hand often let less serious crimes slip by, too often, in Corcoran's view.

"Everything's gonna be green again and we're gonna hear the heifers calling their young clear up here on the mountain," Connor said. "Sun's shinin' down kinda hard this afternoon. Makes one a bit thirsty, eh?"

"Does indeed, Sheriff. Does indeed." Corcoran chuckled, watched Ed Connor toss his tin cup back inside the office, and the two ambled across the main street and turned toward Jimmy Henderson's Bonanza Club. "Cold beer on a hot spring morning should be a job requirement, I'd say."

Terrence is in his thirties, tall and rangy, and wears long reddish hair that hangs in waves. Women are drawn to the man, and he rarely objects to that. His bright-green eyes can be filled with mirth or carry a threat of instant death. Your call. He will tell anyone who will listen that he is as Irish as they come, but the man was born on a boat four days out from Ireland. He's never put a foot down on the emerald isle.

Terrence Corcoran was raised in New York and came west at sixteen. Today he's a fine lawman but worked on railroads as a drover, and it took a few years before he found his calling in the law. The man is proud as hell of wearing a badge.

"Looks like our fine blacksmith has an urge for something cold this morning," Corcoran said, spotting Abe Afeldt standing at the bar. "Mornin' Abe. Our spring is getting even warmer, eh?"

"Ach," he spat. "To hell with spring and to hell with women." Afeldt was a huge man, stood as tall as Corcoran but outweighed him by a hundred pounds or more. He had long, black, straight hair that was showing patches of white here and there. He was a blacksmith, fine carpenter, and those in Eureka called on him to fix anything that broke. Or to lift anything they couldn't.

Come county fair time, Abe Afeldt was sure to win any and all feats of strength—from driving steel in hard rock mining contests to throwing calves in rodeo contests. "This isn't the same Abe Afeldt I've known for a few years," Ed Connor said. "A little woman trouble, Abe?"

"Ach. They smile at you, tease you, then laugh at you when you take their bait. All 'look and no touch' is these creatures. I'll not be friends with the lot of 'em," he snarled. He drained his glass and stomped out of the saloon.

"That ain't like Abe," Corcoran said. He motioned for the Bonanza Club owner, Jimmy Henderson, acting as bartender that fine morning, to bring them some cold beer. "What's with Abe this morning, Jimmy?"

"Maria Castelleno was in last night. Alphonso was at the mine late and she came in, gave Abe the full treatment, big eyes, grand smile, seeming to offer paradise and the damn fool fell for it. They had oysters and champagne and she up and left him with a bill for well over a hundred dollars."

"He's not as bright as some when it comes to women," Connor said. "If he gets to messing around with Alphonso Castelleno's wife, there'll be trouble. She's caused a lot of trouble in the past that way."

Castelleno owned one of the better producing mines in the area, wrenching considerable amounts of gold and silver from the hard rock every month. He was of southern European background, acted the part of a European nobleman, and was known to have killed at least one man who made the mistake of taking advantage of Maria's advances.

"She comes in every time Alphonso has to work late at the mine." Henderson shook his head and poured three beers. "I'll join you, boys." He raised his frosty mug high in the air. "To spring."

"She's in as much danger as Abe if Castelleno hears of this," Connor said. "That man's got a temper. My heavens, man, Castelleno gives her anything she asks for—furs, gems, horses. Woman's being a fool."

"From what I understand," Henderson said, "she's seen at the Eureka House Saloon as well. I've heard that Hatfield has hosted her for quiet dinners in his office more than once."

Gordon Hatfield arrived in Eureka about a year ago, bought the Eureka House Hotel, Saloon, and Dance Hall, and enjoys flashing his wealth. Debonair, somewhat dashing in appearance, the single women in town seem impressed with his velvet tongue and gold coins. It's because of his dashing manner, heavy drinking, and loose morals that the business is known to be failing.

"That's a strange situation over there," Connor said.

"It looks like Hatfield should be making money but he insists he's losing money on the operation."

"If it was my place," Henderson said, "I'd start looking around at those who have control of his money. Those dealers at the tables, the bartenders, even the bookkeeper. The business may be making money, but it isn't reaching his pockets."

Corcoran chuckled. "You've had those troubles in the past, Jimmy. It's too nice a day to be inside." Connor and Corcoran finished their beers and walked out onto the boardwalk to stand in the warm sun.

"Isn't that Hank Sawyer heading into the Eureka House?" Ed Connor pointed at a buckaroo who was passing through the swinging doors at the Eureka House across and down the main street. "You talked to him since we got that wire from Deputy Ainsley in Palisade?"

"Sounds like the right time to me, sheriff," Corcoran said. "Ainsley wasn't positive on the robber being Sawyer, but it won't hurt to bump him around some. Not nice to hit a storekeeper with a rifle butt and take his money." Corcoran stepped off the walkway and headed off toward the big hotel. *Shame the way this old building is falling apart. Always liked the Victorian architecture. Henderson built the Bonanza out of rough wood chinked tight, but all that fancy wood on the Eureka gives it a nice flavor.*

Sawyer was known for working as security for some of the ranches in the Diamond Valley. He was also thought to be responsible for much of the rustling that takes place. He was fast with his fists, knives, and guns, and had a bad reputation with store clerks who angered him in some way. Many believed that Hank Sawyer was also responsible for some of the thefts in the county from Palisade on the north to Eureka on the south. There were rumors to the effect that his guns were available for hire at a high price.

―――――

THE EUREKA HOUSE HOTEL and Saloon was failing when Gordon Hatfield bought it, and it was now evident that things hadn't gotten better. Corcoran eased through the bat-wing doors and took a look around the long and narrow saloon.

A few of the oil lamps were lit but didn't offer much light. There were a couple of men at the bar, the piano stool was empty, as was the faro table. Three men were playing poker, one of them being Gordon Hatfield, the owner. Sawyer was standing off to the side as if waiting for a chance to talk with Hatfield.

Corcoran walked to the bar and nodded at the barman for a cold beer. "Nice day," he said.

"Gonna be a scorcher, Corcoran. Be sellin' beer by the barrel," the barman laughed. Tony Soma was nearing fifty, had worked the mines in Virginia City until his left leg was almost crushed in a rockslide, and came to Eureka several years ago. He limped but never complained about his aches and pains.

"Sawyer come in here often, Tony? I thought he was working for the Durbin Ranch up near Palisade."

"Been in several times the last few days. Talks with Gordon and leaves. Nasty sumbitch most of the time.

Takes great pleasure in trying to bump my bad leg when I have to bring him drinks."

Corcoran took a quick look over to Sawyer and back to his beer. *Comes in to talk with Gordon Hatfield, eh? Wonder why? Selling stolen items? Getting paid for some job?* Corcoran moved down the bar so that he could watch Hatfield and Sawyer without it being so obvious.

It was just as Corcoran was ordering his second schooner of beer that Hatfield jumped to his feet, gun in hand, yelling at one of the players. "You bloody cheat! In my own place, at my own table, you cheat in a friendly little game?" He swung the Colt Army and slammed it across the side of Milt Jackson's head, raked in Jackson's chips to his side of the table, and motioned for Hank Sawyer to throw Jackson out of the saloon.

Sawyer grabbed the gambler by the back of his shirt and the seat of his pants and dragged him across the saloon and heaved him through the swinging doors. The other player and Corcoran noticed that many of the table's chips made their way to Hatfield's stash but no one said anything. Corcoran walked over to the table. "Problems, Hatfield?"

"Nothing I need your help with." He motioned for Sawyer to follow him upstairs to his office. "Ain't no reason for the law to get involved. Get on back to your beer, Corcoran. That's what you do best."

Corcoran smiled at the slight but knew he would remember it for a long time. *Have to straighten him out one of these days.* Corcoran looked over at Sawyer with half a scowl on his face. "Thought you were working up Palisade's way, Sawyer. What brings you to the big city?"

"Ain't none of your concern. I'll go wherever I please, deputy."

"Nice chatting with you two," Corcoran said. "I love coming into friendly and warm little businesses in this town. That's a nice holster you're wearing, Sawyer. Get that at Gensler's Gun Store in Palisade, did you?" Jim Gensler was still in the hospital following the attack on the man and there were questions on whether he would ever fully recover. The rifle butt did severe damage to the man's skull.

"Go to hell, Corcoran," Sawyer said and pushed past the deputy, heading for the staircase to join Hatfield.

Corcoran turned for the door hoping to catch up with Milt Jackson. *Interesting that the other man at that table didn't stand up for Jackson or maybe he was pleased by Hatfield's reaction. There was a lot more at play there than five-card stud.*

Jackson was on his feet but groggy when Corcoran stepped out of the Eureka House. "Milt, here, let me help you. How about we find you a cup of coffee, eh?" His head was bleeding and he had scrapes on his face from falling hard on the boardwalk. "You took a pretty nasty swat there."

CHAPTER TWO

JACKSON HAD a hard time with his balance as Corcoran walked the two to the sheriff's office for that coffee. His head was bleeding and his eyes weren't focusing and Corcoran had to catch him on more than one stumble. "Settle in, Milt, and I'll pour us a cup. You work underground at the Castelleno Mine, don't you?"

Jackson wiped some blood from his forehead and shook his head slightly. He was having a hard time getting his eyes to work together but seemed to know he was talking to Corcoran. "Yeah, Corcoran. Second shift. Damn this hurts."

Corcoran found a bowl and got some water in it. "Here, wash your face in this. It'll ease the pain too. Ain't known you for cheatin' at cards. What brought all that on with Hatfield? Ain't known him for bein' that good a player neither," Corcoran chuckled.

"He ain't any kind of player. I don't cheat, Corcoran." Jackson stiffened at the comment and scowled thinking about it. "Never have, never will. Ain't no reason to if you're a good player, and I am one. It was my third win when he blew up. He dealt the hand for Pete's sake. Had my sleeves rolled up. How could I cheat? He took all my winnings, Corcoran. Had a couple of hundred on the table there. He's gettin' good at that."

"This isn't the first time?" Jackson nodded and grimaced at the loss. *Most interesting that our saloon owner is a cheat. Calls a man a cheat, throws him out of the joint and rakes in all the coins. Hadn't heard about this and I'll bet it traces right back to his money problems.*

"Take a deep breath, Milt, and tell me about some of this." Corcoran sat down in Connor's chair at the sheriff's desk, thought about the flask in the third drawer down, and put the thought aside. Just for the time being, you understand.

"When the game ain't going his way, someone gets either beat up or tossed out. Either way, whatever money's on the table goes to Hatfield. Seen it often. Never thought he would call me out, though. I'm gonna bust his head for this, Corcoran. Gonna make that man hurt."

"How about you let me take on that chore, Milt? You play regular? Most mornings?"

"Two, sometimes three times a week," Milt Jackson said. "Most of the time with the regular dealer, Offenhouser. Don't like it when Hatfield's dealing. He's the cheat."

"Is Sawyer usually around? He was kinda rough on you."

"He's Hatfield's dog, Corcoran. Does what he's told to do and gets his bone afterward. Some of my money will end up in his pockets. He ain't got a thought of his own in that ugly head, only does what he's told and then only if he gets paid. He got back in town a few days ago. He and Hatfield got some kind of doins going on. All hush-hush."

———

HATFIELD POURED two glasses of whiskey for himself and Sawyer and motioned for the outlaw to sit down. "Were you able to get those guns that Gensler had?"

"Five brand-new Henrys and a couple of cases of ammunition. What's better, the safe was open and I scooped up a couple of thousand dollars."

Gensler had dealings with the army and with various law enforcement departments in eastern Nevada to provide arms and ammunition. A fat government contract that kept his little shop in Palisade nice and busy. Gensler was a gunsmith by trade and most of the buckaroos in the area bought and traded with the man.

"How'd you get it all here without anyone noticing? That damn Corcoran seems to know what everyone's doing before they do it." Hatfield had heard about run-ins with Terrence Corcoran and believed a lot of the tall tales told about the man. "If we're gonna get that bank taken care of, we gotta get rid of Corcoran first. You got the people we're gonna need?"

Gordon Hatfield was running out of money fast just trying to keep the Eureka House afloat. He moved to Eureka and bought the hotel-saloon complex thinking it was a going concern and since has had to spend most of his wealth just keeping it open. With his acidic personality he couldn't keep help—hotel staff in particular—and didn't have good relations with many in the town. He decided his best bet would be to get a good insurance policy on the hotel, rob the bank, and set fire to the complex.

The money to buy the place came to him when his father passed away. The elder Hatfield was a successful New Orleans gambler, but his son never learned the ins and outs of the games. As a businessman, he ran a poor third to Jimmy Henderson at the Bonanza Club, whose enterprise seemed to be filled at all hours. Henderson's hotel rooms were clean, linen was clean, and fresh water was always available. His restaurant served the best food in central Nevada, and his gaming tables were honest. None of which could be said of Hatfield's operation.

"I had a wagon and team tethered behind Gensler's place," Sawyer continued. "After I whacked him I locked the doors and pulled the shades. Emptied the place right out the back door," he laughed loud at his own comment. "I pulled into town just before dawn today and have the rifles and stuff at the barn. I need to get back to the ranch before they find out I've been gone for three days. Supposed to be riding the north section, looking for Indian rustlers."

"Indian rustlers?" Hatfield laughed loud and poured them some more whiskey. "You're the one been doing the rustling. Haw-haw." He sat back in his leather chair and laughed some more. "Any problems selling those steers?"

"Not since you made those running irons to alter the brands," Sawyer said. "All I do is move a few head at a time to that canyon, the boys alter the brands and drive them to market. When should I bring the boys to town?"

"Next big shipment from the Reno banks will be here in ten days, Hank. You and the boys need to be here at least two days before that. I've got the dynamite. When they move that shipment from the railway to the bank, we'll hit 'em hard. You know where to take the boys and the money."

"Sure, Gordy. Got that cabin all ready for us. There's food, rifles are in the barn." He stood up and finished his drink. "I gotta go. I'll be back with the boys."

He slipped out of the office and made his way downstairs, Hatfield sat at his desk with a smile spread across his face. *It's finally falling into place. I really thought this old saloon would be my rainbow but it's gonna be the Eureka Bank's instead. Pay those dolts off and make my way to Mexico and a life of leisure. Señoritas, tequila, and sunshine all put together and held in place with many thousands of dollars in good old American gold. It would be considerably better if I didn't have to split with Sawyer and those other dolts.*

He smiled for just a moment or two. *On the other hand, I could kill that Castelleno fool, marry the fascinating Maria, and own the mine. I like having to make these kinds of decisions.*

––––––––––––––

AN HOUR or so after Milt Jackson left the office, Corcoran spotted Hank Sawyer riding out of town and made for the stalls in the back of the courthouse, got his horse, Dude, saddled, and rode west, down toward the

Diamond Valley. The main road continued west but at the railroad station a branch turned north.

"Happen to see which way Hank Sawyer rode?" Corcoran asked one of the railway workers. "Should have passed by just a few minutes ago."

"Ya, Terrence. He went north by golly. You can catch if you hurry."

"Thanks, Sven," Corcoran said putting Dude in a strong trot north. *What would the Eureka House owner be involved in that he would enlist the likes of Hank Sawyer? Sawyer's the kind of man you would hire as a guard or someone for protection. He isn't any kind of thinking man. He would be the muscle not the brain in any outfit.* Corcoran had to chuckle thinking about it. *Hatfield sure ain't much for brains either.*

He made a fast five miles and saw Sawyer on the trail a quarter mile or so in front. Corcoran urged the big horse on a little and slowly caught up with the outlaw. "Hold up, there, Mr. Sawyer. Got a couple of questions for you."

Sawyer spun in the saddle and immediately went for his sidearm. He was slow and clumsy, and Corcoran pulled and fired before Sawyer got his pistol clear of leather. Sawyer took a large chunk of hot lead in his arm because of it. The shot knocked him right out of the saddle, his revolver flying off into the dirt and rocks. Corcoran stepped down from Dude, picked up the gun, and aimed it at the outlaw's face.

"Stupid, Sawyer. All I wanted to do was ask a couple of questions. Now you're going to jail with a charge of attempted murder of a law man. You're just as dumb as you look, mister." Corcoran spent the next few minutes getting the bleeding stopped and wrapped, using ripped pieces of Sawyer's own clothing. He relieved the man of a large knife at his belt and pulled the fine leather holster off as well.

"Still has the price tag on the back, Sawyer. You really are as stupid as you look." He held it up to Sawyer's face. "See? Right there. It says, Gensler's leather works, five dollars. Charges are starting to pile up my friend. What were you and Hatfield talking about?"

"Ain't none of your concern," Sawyer said. "My business is my business."

"Why'd you try to shoot me? That is my business." Corcoran laughed, reached out and poked his fist into Sawyer's wounded arm, getting a scream of pain from the man. "Maybe now you'll give me an honest answer, eh?"

Sawyer clammed up and refused to answer. "Okay then, let's get you back to town. Onto your horse now," he said. He jerked the man to his feet and got him in the saddle and tied securely. "We'll ride back nice and slow," Corcoran said. "What were you and Hatfield talking about before you left town? Or were you just getting your cut of Jackson's winnings?"

"Ain't got nothing to say to you, Corcoran. The business that me and Hatfield have is none of your business."

"Well, Mr. Sawyer, that's where you're wrong. Being a deputy sheriff means that whatever business you and Hatfield have just might be unlawful business, and that would make it my business." He reached across the distance between the men and poked the wound again. Sawyer, his hands tied behind him and his legs tied together under the horse, tried to kick the horse forgetting that Corcoran held the lead rope.

Corcoran let the horses run for a minute and then pulled them up short, turning hard to the right. Sawyer toppled from the saddle but couldn't fall because of his feet being tied together. He was screaming in pain and fear as the horse picked that moment to throw a fit. Sawyer was hanging upside down, getting kicked in the head with front feet, back feet, and being bounced off the rocks every time the horse jumped.

Corcoran was laughing at the sight but got the horse settled quickly, got Sawyer freed and on the ground, and stood over the frightened man, a huge fist doubled and ready to smash meat and bone.

"Yes, Mr. Sawyer, what you were talking about is my business." He got all the ropes straightened out, got the man back on the spooked horse and retied, and started again for Eureka. "I've got enough evidence to have any judge in Nevada tuck you away in Carson City for a long time, mister. Wearing stolen property, trying to shoot a deputy, and attempted escape. Give that some thought, let it seep into that big stupid head and then I'm going to ask some more questions."

At a walk it was a long time getting back to the sheriff's office and Corcoran was no more educated than when he left. Sawyer refused to answer any questions, did some whimpering from time to time, particularly when Corcoran thumped his wounded arm, but said nothing. Corcoran put him in a cell and sent jailer Tommy Reilly to fetch the doctor.

"Man won't say a word, Sheriff," Corcoran said

coming back into the main office. He spent the next half hour telling Connor about his time at the Eureka House and the capture of

Sawyer. "There's something cooking between Sawyer and Hatfield but we're not going to find out what it is from Sawyer."

Corcoran wanted to continue the conversation, but two quick shots rang out. "That came from the Bonanza Club, Ed," Corcoran said. He dashed out the door and raced across the street toward the big hotel-saloon, the sheriff just a few steps behind him. He burst through the swinging bat-wing doors and found Jimmy Henderson wrestling for a pistol held by Alphonso Castelleno. It was still smoking when Corcoran grabbed it and wrenched it from both men's hands.

Connor pulled Henderson from the big mine operator and got the two slightly calmed down. "All right, you two. Sit down, both of you," Connor said. "What the hell's going on?"

"Touch my wife and I kill," Castelleno growled. "No man touch my Maria." The man's English wasn't very good under the best of circumstances, and after several strong drinks it got worse. "You stinkin' whore monger."

Corcoran looked at Jimmy Henderson who was ready to jump on the mining magnate and started to chuckle, grabbing everyone's attention. "What the hell's so funny?" Henderson asked. "You want to be called names like that? I've never touched that woman, would rather she not even come in my place."

Corcoran grinned, looked back and forth at Henderson and Castelleno. "He doesn't know where he is, Jimmy. He thinks you're Hatfield and that he's at the Eureka House." Corcoran reached down and helped Alphonso to his feet. "Take it easy, Castelleno, nice and easy. Let's get this straightened out before someone gets hurt."

Corcoran motioned for Henderson to set one of the overturned tables back up and got the miner in a chair. "Sit down, Jimmy, let's talk some." He looked at Alphonso Castelleno and shook his head. The man's eyes weren't focused on anything. "Do you know where you are?"

"Of course I know where I am. I'm here to kill that foul man what touched my wife. Hatfield, you're going to die. Let go of me, Corcoran."

"Well," Corcoran laughed, "at least he knows who I am. Does he have these problems often, Jimmy?"

"When he's drinking someone has to take him home. He doesn't seem to remember where he lives or who he's talking to. Not a good drinker." Jimmy Henderson got up and started back to his bar. "Best get him out of here before he hurts someone."

"Better get a pot of coffee going, sheriff, this might take some time getting our lead mining man sobered up," Corcoran laughed, getting the gentleman to his feet. "Back to the office with us."

CHAPTER THREE

SHERIFF CONNOR and Terrence Corcoran were having supper at the Bonanza Club café, after a busy and long day. "Think the town will survive the night, sheriff?"

"Anything else goes wrong and I'm moving out," Connor laughed. "How did your discussion with Castelleno go?"

"Henderson was right, Ed. The man shouldn't drink. He's filled with jealousy, is aware that his wife has been seen in the saloons when he's on night shift, and, if he gets his way, somebody's going to die because of it. It would have been Hatfield if Castelleno hadn't got drunk and forgot where he was. Jealousy is a terrible price to pay to be married to a charmer like Maria."

"His money won't keep her at home? He should just turn her loose," Connor said. "He's gonna end up losing her anyway."

"Really, he already has lost her. It isn't money she craves, sheriff."

"No?"

"No. It's the excitement of being pursued, getting one over on her husband, and the thrill of having an affair with someone like Hatfield, always the ultra-gentleman while torching someone else's marriage."

"I was right," Connor said. "How could you call that a marriage? He should just dump her, get on with life. Why kill someone over something that's already lost? Stupid if you ask me."

"And dangerous," Corcoran said. "Ain't much we can do about it, though. Just keep an eye out for the man. Can't tell Mrs. Castelleno or Mr. Hatfield not to do it," he chuckled. "Ain't our job to keep marriages together. Castelleno is lucky that Henderson didn't press charges and I told him so in no uncertain terms."

"Good. We need to think about what it is that has drawn Hatfield and Sawyer together," Connor said. "Hatfield's driven that big hotel complex into the ground. He looking to make some fast gold? The wrong way?"

"My first thought," Corcoran said. "Maybe we should have our after-dinner drinks at the Eureka House, eh?"

"The only thing I have against spring is mud, Corcoran," Connor said, evading a large puddle as they crossed the main street. "Another couple of weeks and we'll see green but right now, mud."

"You're a romantic soul, Ed," Corcoran laughed. They made their way to the long bar and ordered brandy. Compared to the Bonanza Club the Eureka House was almost empty. No one playing the piano, only one gaming table active, and a few men at the bar.

"Tony," Corcoran said, "You're working a long shift today."

"Hatfield's got us on twelve-hour shifts. This is probably my last one. Can't work for that man. Changes his mind every half hour of the day, I think." Tony Soma had been a barman since he left the mines and was among the best. "Man simply doesn't know how to treat people. In this line of work treating your customers right is the only way to success. You can buy liquor anywhere, it's how you get treated that brings you back. Hatfield's in the wrong business."

"What's going on with him and Hank Sawyer? That's a strange friendship." Corcoran lit a cigar and took a drink of brandy. "Used to drink this with coffee in my days in Virginia City."

"That when you shot the sheriff, Corcoran?" Soma asked.

"Never mind that," he laughed. "What's with Hatfield and Sawyer?"

"Here comes Hatfield now," Soma said. "I'll let you ask him yourself."

"What are you two doing in here?" Hatfield didn't bother to say hello and didn't seem to want their business as he came up to the bar. "They pay for these drinks, Soma?"

"Of course we paid," Connor said. "I'm the elected sheriff of Eureka County, Mr. Hatfield. It's part of my job to see to it that you can remain in business safely and without fear, not to suck you dry."

"Speaking of safe, Hatfield, Castelleno was looking for you earlier today," Corcoran said.

"That old fool? Married to a beautiful woman and

doesn't know how to treat a real lady. Why would he be looking for me?" Hatfield asked.

"Seems he believes you've been treating his beautiful wife as a whore, Hatfield. He was looking to kill you but got sidetracked by a bottle of whiskey." Corcoran drained his brandy and motioned for Tony Soma to pour him and the sheriff another, flipping a gold coin onto the bar. "By the way, we're holding Hank Sawyer on some serious charges. Stupid man tried to shoot me earlier today and was in possession of stolen property too."

Hatfield's immediate anger told the two lawmen that he was not prepared for that kind of news. "We'll see about that," Hatfield said. "What's his bail? I'll pay it right now."

"That would be up to the judge," Ed Connor said. "He'll have a hearing tomorrow morning at ten. Is he on your payroll?"

"Why would you ask a question like that? Why would it be any of your concern?" Hatfield's anger was starting to show, and Corcoran tensed up just a bit. He glared at Corcoran, his fists doubled up, his chin jutted out as if he was ready to throw a punch. "What do you mean I treated Maria Castelleno like a whore. I've treated her as a lady, always. You can't talk to me like that. You have no right to ask about my dealings with Sawyer."

"I'm asking because it's something the judge might want to know if he's even going to allow bail." Connor fired back. The lawman had a slight smile, maybe it was a smirk, as he stared down the saloon owner. "Everything's a personal attack on you, isn't it? Well, having private dinners with another man's wife is not how I see someone being treated like a lady, Mr. Hatfield."

Corcoran watched the man closely as anger flushed through his face. Would he swing on the big deputy? Would he dare draw on him? Or would he slink off and take it out on an employee or some other customer? Hatfield spit out, "I'll see you in court," spun on his heel and stomped off up the stairs to his office.

"We should have our after-dinner brandies here more often, sheriff." Corcoran smiled, watching Hatfield walk off, motioned for Tony to pour two more. "Makes for a most enjoyable evening."

———

"THIS IS why I love spring mornings in these beautiful mountains we live in," Corcoran said. He and the sheriff were sitting at a table in the Bonanza Club restaurant, looking out the window at the tall mountains surrounding the little mining camp. Cindy Cook had been in his lap, hugging him close while he ordered and was about to descend on him again with a big steak and fries for his breakfast.

Cindy was in her mid-twenties, tiny but vivacious, full of energy and had marriage to Corcoran in her thoughts daily. She ran the kitchen and restaurant at the Bonanza Club with an iron fist demanding the best meats, usually game meat, but often fresh pork, lamb, and of course Diamond Valley beef.

"You didn't come over last night like you promised, Terrence. That wasn't nice." She was pouting as she put his platter down, ran her hand through his long wavy hair, and sighed. "Not nice to treat your lady that way." Sheriff Connor was having a hard time keeping his chuckles under control and Corcoran needed to get out of the conversation.

"Have court this morning, sweetie," he said. "Had to prepare and when it got too late, I just went back to the cabin. Why don't we get together tonight? I'll make it up to you." His smile buckled her knees, and she almost danced her way back to the kitchen.

"Is she going to remember that I'm having breakfast?" Connor growled and Corcoran chuckled. "Why don't you just up and marry that pretty little girl?"

"Think Hatfield will show up at the courthouse?" Corcoran ignored Connor's comment. "I shouldn't have gotten him so angry. Should have been a little more subtle in asking about him and Sawyer. His immediate response finding the man in our custody sure got my attention."

"Not gonna talk about gettin' married, eh? You're right though, about Hatfield. He and Sawyer do have something going. He wants that man out of jail. Think he'd do something stupid at court?"

"He is stupid but not that bad," Corcoran said. "No, the judge is safe. If Sawyer gets bail, I'm going to follow him like his shadow, Ed. Maybe we can learn something."

Cindy did bring Connor his breakfast and gave Corcoran a hug and kiss before running back to the kitchen. "She would follow you into the flames of Hades, my friend," the sheriff said. "What kind of business would draw Hatfield and Sawyer together?"

"Illegal," Corcoran said. "Hatfield is going to lose the Eureka House. He needs money in the worst way, Ed. Sawyer is a goon, is a hired goon, so whatever they have going, it's going to be illegal. Court's in an hour. I better get Sawyer ready."

"Does he have an attorney? Interesting isn't it, that Hatfield didn't ask that question?" Ed Connor sopped up pork chop gravy with a big buttermilk biscuit before continuing. "Sawyer's arm going to give him trouble?"

"Ed Graves is with him right now and the doc says his wound is going to heal just fine." Graves was one of just two attorneys in Eureka, the other being the district attorney. "This should be a quick hearing this morning." Corcoran got up and left Connor to finish his breakfast. The jaunt to the office was quick and the attorney, Graves, said Sawyer was ready for court.

"I'll see you at the courthouse, Corcoran. See to it that he gets there in one piece." Graves said that Hatfield hired him to represent Sawyer. "You're mighty handy at whipping on prisoners."

Corcoran ignored the comment and he and the jailer, Tommy Reilly, brought Sawyer out after the attorney left. He had his hands cuffed behind his back and was wearing leg-irons as well. The sheriff's office and jail were down the street from the courthouse, on the downhill side. It was just a short walk on a fine morning. A few people were out, gave quick glances at the prisoner being escorted up the hill, but there was no attempt by anyone to interfere.

CHAPTER FOUR

"GOOD MORNING," Justice of the Peace Thomas Trimble said, sitting down behind his high bench. He opened a notebook, looked around the room, and got things started. "Our first case this morning is an initial hearing dealing with an attempted shooting. The case of Eureka County Deputy Sheriff Terrence Corcoran and one Henry Sawyer. Deputy Corcoran and Eureka County are represented by District Attorney Phelps and Mr. Sawyer by Attorney Graves."

On the frontier some courthouses were thrown-together affairs but the Eureka County building was substantial, built of local quarried rock and sitting on bedrock. Oak, mahogany, maple, and other woods were used throughout as well as Italian marble. The district courtroom was fully paneled with imported maple. On this morning there were less than ten spectators in for the proceedings, some just to get warm not caring a tinker's damn about Hank Sawyer.

Judge Trimble looked out across the courtroom.

"Mr. Phelps are you ready?" Phelps nodded and mumbled something. "Mr. Graves?" Graves said yes loud and clear. "Good. Let's get it on, Mr. Graves. These are serious charges. Your client is charged with attempting to shoot a lawman, attempted escape, and being in possession of stolen property. How does he plead, sir?"

"Not guilty, Your Honor, and we ask that he be released on bail at once. Mr. Sawyer is not safe being held in the same jail in which Deputy Corcoran works. Corcoran shot the man and brought him into custody after a thorough beating."

"Your Honor, if I may," Phelps said, and the judge nodded. "We ask that Mr. Sawyer be held without bail. Yes, he was shot by Deputy Corcoran after Mr. Sawyer attempted to shoot him. His bruises and cuts were suffered from his falling off his horse. There was no beating."

"Who would be putting up the bail if I offer it?" Trimble asked.

"Gordon Hatfield, an upstanding businessman in Eureka, Your Honor," Graves said. Ed Connor coughed softly at the comment, but the judge let it go. He did notice the quirk of a smile from Corcoran.

"I'll grant bail of one thousand dollars cash money and there are restrictions. Mr. Sawyer you are not to leave the township of Eureka between today and trial. Mr. Graves, you will be responsible to see to it that that order is fulfilled. Do you agree to that, Mr. Sawyer?"

"I got a job up in the valley. Can't just sit in this rotten town."

"If you want to be out on bail you will obey the rules, sir. Will you?"

Graves had some strong words with Sawyer, not loud enough for the rest of the people in the courtroom to hear, but Sawyer straightened right up. "I'll stay in town," he said.

Trimble opened his notebook again, made a couple of notations and looked out over the room. "Trial will be in two weeks, the twenty-third, ten o'clock in the morning. Any questions?" No one spoke up and Trimble whacked his gavel. "Sheriff, please release the prisoner and Mr. Graves, bring one thousand dollars, cash money, to my clerk. We're through here."

———

"INTERESTING THAT HATFIELD wasn't in court even though it was his money that was used for bail," Connor said as he and Corcoran strolled back to the office. "What's your plan?"

"I've got little Billie Humphries watching Sawyer right now and I will take over as soon as I get these irons put away. It looked like the man was headed for the Eureka House along with Graves when we left the courthouse."

Corcoran tucked the leg-irons away, poured a quick cup of coffee, and plunked himself down across the table from the sheriff. "We need another deputy, Ed. I don't think Billie's up to it. He's okay as a fill-in night jailer from time to time, but not as a deputy."

"I'm bringing Lou Foster in, Terrence. He'll be a good

one. Big as you are, tough as nails, and wants to be a lawman."

"Good," Corcoran said. "Good man." He put the cuffs up, poured another half a cup of coffee, and was about to take a long drink when Rosita Reynaldo Chavez rushed into the office. "Please, come. Help. Please," she wailed, all but throwing herself at Corcoran. Rosita Chavez was Alphonso Castelleno's housekeeper and along with being more than distraught, was muddy and had cuts and bruises on her arms and face.

"My God, Rosita, what is it?" Corcoran said, getting her arms unwrapped from him. "Here, sit down. Let me get you some coffee. Slow down and tell us what has you so upset. What's happened?"

"It's Mrs. Castelleno. She's dead. Horrible. Help," she wailed. She spilled some coffee that Corcoran handed her, crying, sobbing about a man with a knife. A man who wore a mask. A man who slammed Mrs. Castelleno in the face with a rock.

"Where?" Corcoran asked and Rosita said in the meadow near the Eureka Canyon on the east side of town. "Take me there," he said. He looked at Connor. "Find little Billie and find out where Sawyer and Hatfield are."

Corcoran had Rosita by the arm, and they made the long hike to the lovely meadow just outside of town. It took less than fifteen minutes for the walk and Rosita led him to the crumpled body of Maria Castelleno. A horse and empty buggy were standing on the edge of the meadow.

The lady was known for her ravishing beauty, always

dressed to show it off, and was a flirt, egging men on. Corcoran was looking at a horribly mutilated face, the bloody rock responsible was on the ground alongside. "You said the man was wearing a mask?" Rosita nodded, trying her best not to look at the body.

"What else can you tell me? Do you have any idea that you might recognize or know the man?"

"No. He never said a word, just hit her over and over. I ran and he chased me, knocked me down, kicked me, and then, like he heard something, ran off. He was maybe this tall," and she held her hand a few inches above her head. "Not heavy but not skinny either."

Corcoran looked Rosita over, saw the scratches on her arms, bruises as well, and the fact she had a black eye. *Interesting,* he thought, *that the man would kill Maria and only beat up Rosita. Maria is mutilated while Rosita was only slightly pummeled.*

"Eyes? Did you see what color? What color hair?" Corcoran wasn't getting much help. When this level of violence is taking place right in front of someone, little things like eye and hair color are often not seen. "What kind of clothing did he have on?"

Rosita was crying, had sank to the grass, shaking her head. "I don't know. I think he had maybe black hair. Black suit with white shirt."

Corcoran looked around the open meadow and saw a blanket laid out, a couple of baskets, and a small one-horse carriage. "Were you and Maria having a picnic?"

"Yes. She said it was a wonderful day for a picnic and had me make some fried chicken, some biscuits, and some chocolate cake. It's all in the baskets."

"Enough for the two of you?" Corcoran couldn't imagine that if she was meeting someone, she would have brought Maria along, yet how else would someone know where to find her? Unless it was Alphonso in the mask.

"There is a lot of food. She's gone on picnics before but never asked me to come along. Unusual," Rosita said.

"Do you think she was looking to meet someone here?" Corcoran was going through the baskets and found more than enough food for three. *A man wearing a mask, dressed in a black suit, knowing Maria would be here in the meadow. Alphonso wears black suits when he's doing mine business. Gordon Hatfield wears black suits often.* Corcoran was working his way through some of the men in Maria's life. *I've never seen old Abe Afeldt in any kind of suit. Doesn't mean he doesn't have one.*

He bent down next to the body hoping to find something the man may have dropped or that Maria may have ripped away. Her hands were empty, fingernails clean, bodice not ripped, nor were there any bruises on her neck. Just the gruesome destruction of her face and head.

She didn't rip his clothing, didn't scratch his eyes out, and it doesn't look like she had time to fight back at all. He called Rosita over. "When did you first see the man? Tell me how this all happened."

"I was spreading the blanket and Maria walked over here to pick some of those flowers there. The man came running from those trees with the rock and just attacked her."

Corcoran walked the ten feet or so into the stand of trees, saw where the rock had been lifted from the damp ground, and saw prints that looked very much like boot prints, not shoe prints. He found a length of twig and laid it along a print, cutting it to size.

"Can you drive the carriage?" he asked.

"Oh, yes. I often drive Maria. She's not good with animals."

If that's the case, why didn't you use the carriage to come report the killing? Corcoran had at least another hundred questions that wouldn't be answered right away.

"Take the carriage and stop at the doctor's and tell him to come out and meet me here, then go home and find Mr. Castelleno and give him the bad news. Can you do that?"

"Of course," Rosita said.

"One other thing. Did you or Maria tell anyone that you were coming for a picnic? Anyone at all?"

"Only little Pedro in the stables, you know, to get the horse and carriage ready. Maybe Sabrina in the kitchen to help me pack the food. That is all," Rosita said. She thought about it and continued. "We stopped at the market for some fresh apples and Maria told the lady what we were doing."

"Thank you, Rosita. Don't forget to send the doctor out. It's very important." She nodded, got the horse untied and drove off for town. *Why didn't she bring the carriage to get me? Distraught?* He knew she would be sobbing for most of the trip. He tried to remember whether she and Maria had been very close. Corcoran spent several minutes going over the footprints in the soft ground around the trees, letting his mind go to work while he waited for the doctor.

"Besides Abe Afeldt did Maria tempt any others in

our fair city?" Corcoran caught himself talking out loud and looked around to make sure he was alone. Hatfield and Afeldt had come to mind immediately as did George Florencio. Florencio was a hunter and provided the Bonanza Club with deer, antelope, elk, and bear meat. His wife ran the meat market, but Corcoran knew he had wandering eyes and had been in more than one affair with young and pretty women.

Corcoran mumbled to himself trying to picture how someone would know Maria would be here. The man had to be working from a plan, had to know she would be here, have time to get a mask on, and wait for his chance standing in a grove of trees. Was he invited? Was she waiting for someone else and the killer knew it? One other question came to mind, and it worried him. Why wasn't Rosita killed?

"I know Castelleno was more than upset with Maria, but was he even more upset with Hatfield? Hatfield was not in court this morning. Is he dead somewhere too? Or, if Hatfield did this, is Castelleno dead somewhere? Or Afeldt? Damn," Corcoran found himself talking out loud and looked around again with a sheepish look on his face to see if anyone was listening.

"Did this woman have other love interests or was she flirting or taunting any other men in town?" He had no answers and saw Doc Whidby coming into the meadow. Whidby walked right up to the body and knelt, shaking his head.

"There are those in town who have suggested for some time that this was going to happen," the doctor said. "Think it was her husband, Corcoran?"

"Could be any of several that come immediately to mind, Doc. I'm not a speculating type. I'd rather go on evidence and right now all I have is a dead woman, a rock that is probably the murder weapon, and a set of footprints in some mud." He looked at the doctor and then at Maria.

"What can you tell me about the wounds? Were they from a strong person, an angry person, a man, or woman? The more you can tell me about how the wounds were inflicted the easier it might be for me to catch the bastard."

"I can tell you straight out, Corcoran, whoever did this was strong, was in a rage, and intended to do as much physical damage as possible. I can't go more in-depth than that. A strong woman could do this, but she would have to be very strong. I'd look for a strong man, probably one who has been hurt by this woman's actions."

What the doctor said did not eliminate Maria's miner husband, the blacksmith, or the hunter but may have put a question in Corcoran's mind about Hatfield. "Thank you, Doc. I now have at least five, maybe six suspects," Corcoran chuckled. "I'll send a wagon out for you."

"I already ordered it," Whidby said. "Again, Corcoran, whoever did this was in a rage. Be careful."

Be careful, eh? Probably the best advice anyone could give. A strong person in a rage, he said. Anger at her for betraying a marriage? For making a fool of him at the bar? For seeing other men? There are as many reasons for a man to go into a rage as there are women. Corcoran pondered that thought and changed his mind.

No, old man, that's what some men believe but I know better. Little Cindy Cook is a perfect example of what a wonderful woman can be. Just the thought of how wonderful some women are brought back memories of Crazy Hair. His love for her and her love for him was about to take him out of the life of a lawman. He was ready to retire, buy a ranch, and raise a family.

No, old man, all women are not like Maria Castelleno. Despite her and Alphonso's relationship, her flirting and teasing, I will find her killer. No one has the right to do what was done to her.

CHAPTER FIVE

CORCORAN WALKED into the Eureka House and found Hatfield and Sawyer talking at the bar. "Need to talk, Hatfield. Alone."

Hatfield was about to tell Corcoran where to go until he looked into the grim and angry eyes. "Let's take a table," he said and walked to one near a front window. "Must be important to drag you away from the Bonanza Club bar."

Corcoran let the slight go by and followed the saloon owner to a table. He took a long look at Hatfield's boots and saw where they were splashed with mud and sat down. "Maria Castelleno is dead." He didn't go any further with the comment, just looked into Hatfield's face as he said it.

"Dead, eh? The old man finally had enough of her? Figured it might happen someday. Why are you telling me?" Hatfield motioned for the barman to bring a bottle over.

"You been in here all morning? You weren't in court." Corcoran said.

Hatfield chuckled and glanced around the almost empty saloon. "No, I wasn't in court and I wasn't here either. Had some chores to take care of. Been here for about an hour or so."

"Were any of these chores done where someone can verify you doing them?" Corcoran noticed mud on the sleeve of his black suit coat. *Interesting that there's mud on his clothing and boots. A thinking man would not have left that.*

"I have a small property in the canyon east of town, Corcoran, and was there to bring some cases of liquor in. I have a solid barn on the property and use it as a warehouse. I was alone so you'll just have to take my word for it."

"Probably not, Hatfield. I don't take anyone's word for anything." The barman brought the bottle over and Corcoran got to his feet. "Enjoy your bottle."

Corcoran hummed a little tune walking the couple of blocks back to the office. *I'll be visiting that solid barn of his very soon. Have to visit Alphonso Castelleno as well. That won't be fun.*

————

CORCORAN HAD FILLED a couple of pages of notes when Sheriff Connor walked in. "We got us a lot to talk about, Terrence. I haven't eaten in seventeen days now, so let's hit the free lunch at the Bonanza Club, eh? Followed Hatfield after Sawyer went into the Eureka House. We got lots to talk about."

"You followed him to a piece of property in the canyon east of town?" Corcoran smiled as he asked. "Did he move some cases of liquor from a well-built barn?"

"How the hell did you know that? Damn, Corcoran. How? You enjoy jerking my chain like that, don't you?" Connor pretended to be hurt but knew that little things like this were why Corcoran was the best.

Corcoran was laughing as he got up, folded his notes into the notebook, and reached for his sombrero. "I'll read these notes to you as we have lunch. I think we're gonna have a hard time finding Maria's killer."

The free lunch buffet consisted of smoked elk, cheeses, and fresh bread and rolls. Jimmy Henderson learned about the idea in Denver where hotels featured the free lunch. To partake, all one had to do was order a drink. It became an immediate success in Eureka.

Corcoran took his time telling Connor what he'd found out at the crime site and at the Eureka Hotel. "We have a number of possible suspects, Ed. Castelleno, Hatfield, Afeldt. Maybe one or two we don't know about yet. Tell me what you found out."

"Well, first off, Hatfield was exactly where he told you he was. That doesn't rule him out though. I followed him to that barn he told you about but when he left, I stayed to see what I could find out about the place. He's implicated in the Gensler robbery in Palisade, and more."

"He was with Hank Sawyer?" That surprised Corcoran. "Didn't think the man had it in him."

"Maybe not right there, but implicated. I found five brand-new Henry rifles that were part of what Sawyer stole. Those two are definitely up to something big.

Several cases of dynamite and blasting caps as well. Whatever they're after, it's big."

"As big as a bank maybe?" Corcoran asked and Connor chuckled at the thought. "We need to keep eyes on that barn, Ed. Was the area muddy? Whoever killed Maria was in a muddy area before the killing and Hatfield's boots had mud on them."

"So do mine right now," the sheriff said. "It's muddy out there. Do you think he stopped on the way back and waited for Maria?"

"Somebody did," Corcoran said. "I'm not ruling Hatfield out at all, Ed. I want to swing by the blacksmith's and have a chat with Abe. He was incensed the other day and Doc Whidby said whoever killed Maria was in a rage." Corcoran paused, wondering about Hatfield. *He was riding a horse, but I didn't see any hoof prints anywhere around that stand of trees.*

"I think it's time for young Mr. Foster to learn the ropes of being a deputy sheriff. I'll put him on barn watch." Ed Connor had hired Lou Foster as a trainee deputy and was using him more for jailer duties than out on the streets. "He's ready."

AFELDT'S STABLES and blacksmith shop were down in the gulch on the north side of town and Corcoran found the big man cleaning the hooves of a fine-looking Morgan stallion. "Nice horse, Abe. Who's the lucky man?"

"That bastard, Castelleno," Afeldt growled. "Ah, nuts. I don't hate him, but that woman he's married to is a horrible person." He stood up and ran his hands all over the strong horse. "Bet this big boy can work all day and still want to play come night. Ah, well, so be it for us single men."

"That's why I'm here, Abe. Maria Castelleno was killed this morning." He watched Abe slowly let his hands come away from the horse's neck. "You were upset the other morning when we talked. Have you been here all morning?"

"Had plans to do some fishing later, but as far as this morning goes, I fixed Mrs. Donovan's fence and talked with Sam Benton about his wagon. Wood's all rotted out from him moving so much manure. Why, Corcoran? You think I'd kill someone?"

"It's my job, Abe." Corcoran tried to smile but the situation wasn't right for that. "Whoever did kill Mrs. Castelleno was in a hateful mood, as you were. I'm sure Mrs. Donovan and old man Benton will vouch for you." Abe nodded but did not smile either.

Corcoran took just a moment to look into Abe Afeldt's eyes before continuing. "You said the other day that Mrs. Castelleno flirted and carried on with more than just you. Who might the others be?"

"Florencio for one," Abe said. "Old George was led down the path too. He swore he'd never talk to the woman again. How does Mr. Castelleno feel about his wife leading on all these men? I'd think he'd be a suspect, too, Corcoran."

"No one is a suspect, yet, Abe, but I do plan to have a talk with the gentleman." He said his goodbyes and took a long walk back to the office. Mrs. Donovan showed him the fence and Benton cussed some at how much Abe planned to charge to rebuild the old manure spreader. "Looks like a good time to ride out to the Castelleno Mine property," he mumbled heading for the courthouse stables to saddle his horse, Dude.

William Phelps, Eureka County district attorney was in the stables as well. "Nasty business, Corcoran. Sheriff Connor brought me your report. She's played her little charade with too many of Eureka's men. Should have seen this coming. Where are you heading? To arrest Castelleno?"

"Don't have enough evidence to arrest anyone, Bill. Why do you think

Castelleno is responsible?"

"Pretty much a natural assumption, I'd think," Phelps said. "I know I'd be in a rage if my wife acted that way. Carrying on with any man who would buy drinks, teasing about things that might happen, then walking off. Castelleno has to be high on your list."

Corcoran watched Phelps ride out of the barn and got Dude out for a good brushing. *The way he's acting I wonder if our fine DA isn't one of Mrs. Castelleno's victims? Might want to be a little careful how I share information on this killing. Not like him to jump to conclusions like that.*

CHAPTER SIX

"I UNDERSTAND the man is upset, Rosita, but I must insist on seeing him." Corcoran made the short ride to Castelleno's home on the mine site only to be told that the gentleman wasn't in any mood to see anyone. The Castelleno house sat above the mine property and had a fine view of the southern Diamond Valley from a large, covered porch. The home was large and had several bedrooms despite the fact the couple was childless.

Rosita Chavez was crying when she came to the door and did what she could to hide her face. "What was his reaction when you told him about the murder?" Corcoran was going to get answers after the ride out, either from the old man or his help.

She took her hands away and Corcoran saw red splotches on her cheeks and a definite black eye. It looked like her nose had been bleeding as well. "He went into a rage, beat me, and then collapsed. He hasn't moved since." She stepped back. "He's on the floor in the great room. I'll be moving to the hotel. He fired me, said it was my fault." She was crying, heaving great sobs, trying to hide the bruises.

Corcoran slipped through the door and found the European gentleman curled in a fetal position in front of the fireplace. The long and lean deputy couldn't take his eyes off the muddy boots nor put away the words Rosita used. *He went into a rage, she said. The same phrase that Doc Whidby used. The same phrase Bill Phelps used.*

Corcoran spent a few minutes trying to get Castelleno awake to no avail. He noticed the man's hands were gnarled and rough, as a man's hands would be after so many years working underground. He wasn't wearing riding boots, though. He had high, laced up work boots on.

If the man who attacked Maria was wearing those types of boots Rosita would have told me. I'm not willing to give this angry old man a pass yet, but this is something on his side of the ledger. After another couple of tries at getting the man up, Corcoran gave up. *Is he feigning?*

"When did Maria tell you that you would be going on a picnic?" he asked Rosita. "Did you put the basket of food together?"

"She told me as soon as Mr. Castelleno left for the mine and said that she wanted enough food for three."

"Any idea who that third person might be? This is very important, Rosita. She was expecting someone to join you. Was it the killer?"

"I don't know," Rosita wailed. "I don't know." Rosita was sobbing, gave the impression her knees would buckle, and Corcoran reached out and steadied her. "I have to leave," she said, pulling away.

"How? You can't be planning to walk to town."

"No. I'll use the wagon. If Mr. Castelleno doesn't like it, that's too bad," she said. She smiled for the first time.

Corcoran laughed. "If you think of anything else to tell me about this morning, don't hesitate." He stepped onto Dude's back and made the short ride back to town. *That didn't go well, did it?* He chuckled at the thought. *Castelleno was not simply unconscious. Playing with me isn't a good idea either. He's covering himself by not having to talk to me and she's hiding something as well.*

Thoughts of the old man beating on Rosita played on Corcoran's mind, and the old man feigning being unconscious added to his anger. Corcoran lived with one simple thought when it came to how a woman should be treated, and it did not include beatings. "I've always believed it's a sick man who feels he has to hit a woman. Every woman should be treated as a lady until she indicates she would rather not be."

It was a simple philosophy and one many men have found out about the hard way. "We learned one thing, Dude." He called out to his horse. "Beating on Rosita told us he could very well have been the man who killed Maria. Hatfield strikes me as one who might strike a woman too. As angry as Afeldt was, he isn't the type of man to beat on a woman." He had several conversations with Dude on the ride back to town.

———

ON ARRIVING IN EUREKA, he saw a group of five men ride in and tie off at the Eureka House. *Strangers passing right by the Bonanza Club and stopping at the obviously run-down Eureka House.* Corcoran turned and put Dude up at the courthouse stables and walked back toward the Eureka House. "Didn't recognize one of them," he mumbled.

Lou Foster stepped out of the sheriff's office as Corcoran came by. "Saw you coming, Terrence. Sheriff wants to talk to you." Foster had worked as a ranch hand but had his eyes on being a lawman for years. He was twenty, almost six feet tall and covered in hard muscle. Corcoran knew he was smart as a whip.

"That badge looks good on you, Lou. You're wearing a heavy piece of responsibility there. Honor that piece of tin, boy." Foster and Corcoran stepped into the office and found Ed Connor in conversation with George Florencio.

"Corcoran, good. Sit down. George was just telling me about something you'll be interested in." Connor looked at the big hunter and nodded. "Go ahead, tell Corcoran what you told me."

"Maybe two days, maybe three, I was coming back through the trees east of town, dropping to the canyon floor, and saw Hank Sawyer and three men drive a wagon to a property that has a big barn on it. Run-down old cabin but a well-built barn. They had a half barrel of powder, some dynamite, and half a dozen beautiful rifles."

"Other than Sawyer, did you recognize any of the men?" Corcoran asked. He looked at Connor. "I just saw five men ride into town and go into the Eureka House. Didn't recognize any of them."

"No, me too," Florencio said. "Not recognize them.

Maybe from Palisade? That where Sawyer is, uh, lives." George's English gets worse if he has to think about it, otherwise he gets along just fine. "Sure would like to have one of those rifles."

"I wonder where those three men are?" Corcoran asked. "You didn't happen to follow them, did you, George?"

"I had my pack mule and was bringing meat to the market, so kept in the trees until I got down to the road. The three men rode past me just as I got to Mama's Market. Don't know where they went."

"Interesting," Corcoran said. "I wonder if those three were a part of the five that just came in?" Corcoran asked knowing he wouldn't get an answer. "Thank you, George. Can't do our job without people like you helping."

Florencio nodded and headed out of the office. "It looks like our friend Gordon Hatfield has either eight men or five men working for him, sheriff. Along with that he has rifles, blasting powder, and dynamite."

"Ain't unusual to have that stuff, Corcoran," Lou Foster said. "We always had that stuff at the ranches where I grew up and where I worked." Foster poured coffee around and had a questioning look on his young face.

"Well, you're right, Lou," Ed Connor said. "Right as can be 'ceptin for one little thing. It's Hatfield's barn and he ain't no rancher. Those men ain't no cowmen neither. That's what makes it unusual and why me and Corcoran are thinking on it as hard as we are."

I shouldn't have let Florencio out without talking about

Maria Castelleno. He's apparently been one of her targets in the past. Corcoran thought as Connor spoke.

Corcoran saw that Lou Foster was quick to understand what the sheriff said and patted the new deputy on the back. "Big lesson there, Lou. Glad you heard it. Let's you and me take a walk up to the Eureka House, eh? See who those yahoos came to town to meet."

CHAPTER SEVEN

THE DAY WAS SLOWLY SLIPPING into twilight as they made their way up the street. The aroma of spring in the Diamond Mountains ebbed and flowed through the crowded streets of Eureka—fresh, with a hint of flowers and grass to it. After long, cold winters, the people swarmed into the great outdoors at every opportunity, and this was one of those special days.

"Do you say hello to everyone, Corcoran?" Foster asked.

"Try to, Lou. Yup, it's a good policy to be as friendly as possible to those good citizens you're supposed to be protecting. You won't find me getting all friendly-like with those that break the law, though." He smiled and tipped his hat to two lovely ladies coming out of a women's hat and shawl store and got grand smiles in return.

"You see, Lou, these people know that I'm here to help them. If I get in trouble with some rowdies, they'll jump right in and give me a hand. If I'm a nasty old bastard, snarling and gruff with the good folk, I'd never get any help."

"There's a lot to this wearing a badge," Foster said. He smiled and tipped his hat to an elderly lady coming out of Johnson's Apothecary and got a smile and nod from her in return. "I like that."

"You're gonna do fine," Corcoran said. They stood on the boardwalk outside the Eureka House for just a moment. "Seven horses at the hitchin' rails, Lou. Men in town mostly walk down to have a cold beer. Let's see who our visitors are."

"That one horse has been ridden hard, Terrence," Foster said, nodding at a sweat-stained bay stud.

"Sure has but you notice none of the others have. Good eye, Lou. Whoever rode it in has probably got a good sweat going as well. Keep that eye working, boy."

There was a goodly crowd in the large but no longer elegant saloon—some at the gaming tables, some crowded around the piano, and one group at the bar surrounding Gordon Hatfield. "Don't be obvious but check that group to see if you know any of them," Corcoran said. "One, the feller in the green plaid shirt, looks familiar but I don't know why."

"He's a hand at the same ranch where Hank Sawyer works. Just south of Palisade." Foster was letting his eyes sweep the bar and saloon as he talked. "Can't remember his name," Foster said. "He's known to get mean when he's drinking. I've heard Pete Ainsley talk about him." Ainsley was the resident deputy in Palisade, the one Sawyer put in the hospital.

"We'll just walk through the place and right back out

and talk about what we've seen," Corcoran said. "So far, no Hank Sawyer."

A buckaroo broke away from the group with Hatfield and walked straight for Lou Foster. He had obviously been drinking heavily most of the day, and stumbled more than once making his way. "You, with the little, tin badge. What are you staring at me for? You ain't got no right to stare at nobody."

"Wasn't staring at you or anyone else, mister. Enjoy your drinks." He turned for the door, but the buckaroo reached out and grabbed his coat. Foster spun and as the man tried to swing a round-house right, Foster let go with one straight from the shoulder. Foster's big fist slammed into the man's nose, crushing it and driving him onto a table where four men were drinking. Two of the men, splashed with whiskey and beer, held the man upright.

"How bad do you want him, deputy?" One of them asked. "If it's all right with you we could teach him some manners."

"Not sure he's in a mood to learn anything," Foster said. "Aim him back at the bar and tell the barman he wants to buy you boys a round." He got guffaws and slaps on the back from a couple of them.

Back out on the street, Corcoran headed toward the Bonanza Club. "Really want a beer after all that," he joked. "You handled that well, Mr. Foster." He got serious quickly as they made their way up the street. "There were four men at the bar in there that I didn't recognize, including the one you told me about."

"He was with other hands from the ranch," Foster

said. "I've been a buckaroo in Eureka County for five years, Corcoran, and not one of them are worth dirtying a rope on. Ain't good hands."

"So, with Hank Sawyer that would make five men probably involved in what it is that Gordon Hatfield is planning," Corcoran said. They walked into the Bonanza Club and found Jimmy Henderson behind the bar. "We could use a couple of cold ones, Jimmy. Did Rosita make it into town okay?"

"She has a room upstairs, Corcoran. She's pretty much bruised up. Wouldn't talk about it. The killer do all that?"

"Probably best for the time being to think that, Jimmy. Let me know if she gets any visitors. While we're thinking about it, Maria stopped at the grocers and bought some fruit for that picnic of hers. Did she get anything here, by chance?" Corcoran remembered that Rosita said there was fried chicken and fresh biscuits but couldn't remember if she mentioned where they came from.

"Has in the past," Henderson said. "Not this time. Usually picks up some sliced meats and cheeses for those picnics. She's never had Rosita along before, though."

"Tell me about some of these other picnics, Jimmy."

"She loves to sit in open meadows, along streams, even from time to time in the mountains, and tease her men friends, Corcoran. She's had picnics with Hatfield more than once, I'm sure. Usually gets enough smoked meat and cheese to make sandwiches for two. Cindy can tell you more about it."

"You mentioned Hatfield. Any others you know of?"

"I'm sure there were," Henderson said, "but I don't know who they would be. Only know Hatfield for sure because he made it obvious. If there were others, they were discreet."

Corcoran grabbed the beers and motioned Lou Foster to join him at a table. "That's a nasty murder to try and solve, Mr. Foster, and I'm almost sure it will be tied in some way to what might be going on with Hank Sawyer and Gordon Hatfield. If you haven't figured it out, you and me are gonna be working mighty close until it's solved."

"I'm looking forward to that," Foster said. He looked out the window and saw Hank Sawyer and four men leave the Eureka House. "Looks like Sawyer and them are leaving, Corcoran. Hatfield ain't with them. He must have just shown up. Come in from the east and we didn't see him."

"Follow, Lou. Be discreet, as careful as you've ever been. Do everything you can possibly do to not be seen. Let me know where they go."

Foster quick footed it to the courthouse stables and saddled up. All he knew was that the group rode out of town toward the east. He was a good ten minutes behind them and simply followed their prints, keeping his ears and eyes at full alert. He was sure the bunch were just walking their horses, not going anywhere fast.

"GLAD THOSE TWO are out of here." Hatfield said. "Man gives me the creeps. Seems to know too much about other people's business."

"Where's Sawyer? He was supposed to be here, Hatfield. Supposed to have guns for us." Mose Willoughby, the man in the green plaid shirt pointed out by Lou Foster, was not in a good mood. "Ain't the best way to get a job started."

"He'll be here, Mose," Hatfield said. "Everything's moving just as I've planned. We'll ride out to the barn in a while, and you'll get your guns. There's a lot of work and planning for an operation like this."

Mose *humphed* some and moved down the bar away from Hatfield. "Don't like the way Hatfield puts us off, Slim. Maybe it be best if you and me pull this job off. To hell with Hank Sawyer and Hatfield. After we get the guns and find out where they have the dynamite stored," he laughed.

Slim Oakley chuckled and turned away from the bar. He had mentioned before that he didn't trust Hatfield, didn't like the barman, Tony Soma, and didn't like drinking at the Eureka House. "Let's you and me take a seat at one of those tables, Mose, and talk about that. This isn't my first bank job, you know, and I know it ain't your first neither."

"Ain't for sure," Mose Willoughby laughed. "Sawyer really fouled up that robbery at Gensler's Gun Store. Deputy up there already sent word to the sheriff down here that he's sure it was Sawyer did the job. We're already being looked at. Saw the big bastard, Corcoran, come in a few minutes ago."

"Yeah, I saw him," Oakley said. "Deputy with him is Lou Foster. Been a buckaroo up north for some time. He's a tough little hombre too. Seen him clear out a bar when somebody tried to cheat him."

"Damn it." Mose snarled. "Hatfield's all flashy and tries to be something he ain't and Sawyer's just a damn bull don't know what he's doing or where he's going. We got to get rid of them and do the job ourselves. We don't need these others either. Just the two of us, a stick or two of dynamite, a good rifle, and we'll empty that bank."

"How do we get rid of Pete and Jake? They're good cow hands but they ain't bank robbers," Oakley said.

"We'll get rid of Sawyer first, then Hatfield. Those two will run for their lives," Mose laughed. "Ain't got much spine anyway. I'll let Sawyer get all angry with me, and you know how easy that is, and I'll take him out in front of the others. I'll leave Hatfield to you."

"Need to take him out secretly, let the sheriff think it's a failed robbery or something. I'm good at that too," Oakley said.

The bottle they took with them to the table was getting empty, helped along by some good-hearted joking when Hank Sawyer walked into the saloon. He nodded to Willoughby and

Oakley as he made his way to the bar to meet with Hatfield. "Time to bring the boys out to the barn, Hatfield. Got everything ready?"

"Good. Call 'em together." Hatfield had a smile on his face thinking what a pleasure it would be to be rid of the Eureka House. "I'll make sure our fire man is ready." The plan was to have the Eureka House burn to the ground while everyone was out at the barn. Hatfield planned to be seen out and away from the building when the fire alarm was sounded.

"The insurance money and the bank's contribution will set me up like a king in Mexico," he muttered, watching Sawyer move through the men to get them out to the barn. *I think it's time for me to pay a visit with my attorney,* Hatfield said to himself. *Ed Graves can verify exactly where I was when the Eureka House burned to the ground.*

CHAPTER EIGHT

OAKLEY HELD BACK when Mose rode out with Sawyer and planned to see to it that the dandy, Mr. Hatfield, had a definite end. He was quick to notice Lou Foster ride out of town several minutes after the others left. *One more good reason for Mose and me to handle this operation. That kid and Corcoran need to be taken care of. Neither Sawyer nor Hatfield know just how dangerous Corcoran can be.*

Oakley's first run-in with Corcoran put the burly buckaroo in Carson City Prison for two years. Oakley knocked a little old lady down and stole some jewelry. When Corcoran tracked Slim Oakley down, the fool tried to whip on the deputy. Oakley spent a week in the hospital before being sent to prison.

Hatfield walked down the main street and turned up toward the courthouse. Lawyer Graves had his office just up the street from the attractive brick building. Oakley jumped on his horse and rode quickly down the street and turned south one block past where Hatfield turned and rode around behind the courthouse.

Landscaping around the proud building added to its attractiveness but also could be used to hide behind if one was planning an assassination. He had his Winchester in hand, tucked down on one knee and took a long sight on Hatfield as he trudged up the hill. *Just another slimy card shark aren't you,* he thought as he squeezed the trigger. Hatfield was less than fifty yards away and the force of the hot lead threw him back at least ten feet. He was sprawled on his back, blood pumping from a neat little hole in the middle of his chest.

All that silk and finery ruined by his own blood, Oakley laughed to himself. He jumped in the saddle and was well away from the scene before anyone came out on the street to see what had happened. Ed Graves was the first to find his client, Hatfield, dead. People milled about for less than two minutes before Terrence Corcoran came sprinting up the street.

"What happened, Mr. Graves? You see this?" Corcoran was breathing heavy after the run.

"No, I was in my office over there and heard the shot." Graves shook his head, looking at the dead gambler. "Heard somebody ride off fast on a horse but never saw anyone. Hatfield hasn't made a lot of friends since moving here, but I didn't know he made this kind of enemy."

Corcoran's first thoughts were of Alphonso Castelleno. He didn't say anything but after Maria's terrible murder, this would certainly fit. Castelleno had already made it known he wanted Hatfield dead. Corcoran sent somebody after Doc Whidby and did his best to keep all the lookers away from the body.

Whidby labored his way up the hill from his office down in the gully and was almost there when the alarms went off. Shouts of "Fire!" made their way up the hill as bells were rung in several sections of the busy mining camp. Nothing was more feared than fire in the mining and ranching villages.

Lumber was the most used building material and the hot, dry summers made it like tinder. Houses and shacks were built close together, and fire equipment was not always the best that could be had. Cisterns were placed for pumpers to draw from, and often the first to arrive only had buckets available to throw water on blasting-furnace flames.

"It's the Eureka House," somebody yelled, and the streets were filled as the throngs arrived for the show. Fire brigades pulled hose wagons and pumpers, bucket brigades were formed, and people got in the way. It was chaos at the Eureka House and Corcoran had to stay with Doc Whidby to protect Hatfield's body.

Sheriff Ed Connor did his best to keep the crowds back and was able to get near one of the pumper captains. "Everybody get out?" he yelled.

"Can't tell, Ed. That place was tinder dry, but I'm sure you're going to be looking at arson. This place was set on fire. I've been fighting fires for fifteen years, sheriff, and I've never seen an entire building catch fire all at once like this one. Whoever lit it had kerosene spread everywhere. It went up like a volcano."

"That's what I'm smelling," Connor said. "Kerosene.

Have you seen Hatfield? I'd think he'd be right here demanding you get the fire out."

"Haven't seen him, sheriff. Might have got himself trapped in there."

"Or might have run off," Ed Connor chuckled. "Let me know if you find anything that might lead me to whoever set this." He started back toward his office, looked up the hill to the courthouse, and saw a group standing in the middle of the street.

That's interesting, he thought, turning up the street. *That's Corcoran and Whidby.* He hurried along as best his bum leg would let him. "Corcoran," he hollered as he got close. *Oh, my god, that's Hatfield on the ground.* "What happened?"

"Shot dead by somebody, sheriff. You down at the fire?"

"Yeah. Eureka House is a total loss. Smiley says he's sure it was a case of arson. What's Hatfield doing up here?"

"We've got ourselves a mess, sheriff. You got this under control, Doc? Let me know what you find. We need a long talk, Ed."

They walked down to make sure things were under control at the fire and turned to the Bonanza Club. "We've got some kind of problem, Ed, and I can't get it straight in my mind." They took their beers into the restaurant and took a table by the windows. Night had fallen, flames were still fifty feet in the air, and the shouting from fire crews echoed up and down the streets.

"Hope they can hold it to just the one building," Connor said. "I've seen whole towns go up in flames. No wind tonight, at least. Is Hatfield's killing related to the fire? Is this the work of Castelleno?"

"It might not have anything to do with either, Ed. Hank Sawyer rode out of town with several men just before Hatfield was killed. Lou Foster is following them. Should be back soon, I hope. Hatfield and Sawyer have some kind of plan that takes several well-armed men and some dynamite. As you said, my first thought is also bank."

"The Eureka Bank is pretty sturdy, Terrence. Rock and brick. If they hit it at night, they would need dynamite but they still wouldn't be able to get that vault open."

"You're right. They can wreck the building and not get at the money. Then again, sheriff, Hank Sawyer ain't the smartest dude around."

———

LOU FOSTER WAS RIDING SLOWLY through the failing light, just far enough behind Sawyer and the others that he could hear their hoof beats but not actually see them. It was a short ride to Hatfield's barn and Foster moved well off the road and got his horse tied off in a stand of trees. He could see lantern light through the boards and windows of the barn and slowly worked his way as close to the building as he dared.

There was no moon. The stars were brilliant in the dark sky, and Foster was near the north side of the barn between some brush and a parked wagon. Even if someone stepped out, he would not be seen. He could hear Sawyer yelling about something and moved right up to the wall just as Slim Oakley rode into the open yard and slid his horse to a stop. Foster got down as low as possible and watched the man make his way inside.

Once inside the barn, Oakley said something to Mose Willoughby but Foster couldn't understand it. Sawyer heard it. Another interruption. "All right, that's enough!" Sawyer yelled out. He was angry and glared at Oakley. "Where the hell've you been? Thought you rode in with us. Now," Sawyer said, "let's talk the Eureka Bank. Hatfield wants us to hit it first thing in the morning. Be there when old man Anderson opens the doors."

Mose Willoughby coughed. "You got a problem with that, Willoughby?" Sawyer had been interrupted for the last time in his opinion. "Spit it out."

"Got a couple of hundred pounds of dynamite, why not just blow the building tonight?"

"And then what?" Sawyer asked. "Do you know the combination to that vault in there? Got the strength to carry it off? This is Hatfield's job and we do it his way. You ride with us or get the hell out now, Willoughby."

Mose jumped to his feet, toppled the bench he was sitting on, and reached for his sidearm. "Bastard," he shouted, drawing slightly faster than Sawyer. Willoughby's aim was true, and Sawyer was flung back with a neat hole in the middle of his chest. His draw, just a bit slower, was not quite on target and the bullet ripped Mose's left ear right off his head, showering Slim Oakley in blood.

The shot's affect was immediate, and Mose crumpled, almost unconscious. Sawyer was dead, and Oakley stood with a gun in his hand. "I think the plan has changed boys," he said. He looked at the two buckaroos Sawyer had brought in. "You ride with me and Mose or leave out now. Ain't no longer Hatfield's job. Mostly because Hatfield ain't around."

Mose Willoughby was slowly getting to his feet, had his neckerchief pushed against where his ear had been, and staggered to a bench. "Almost lost yourself a partner, there, Slim." He tried to laugh and instead just coughed up some blood. The ear canal was bleeding at both ends.

Oakley still had that pistol in his hand and glared at the two men. "Decision time, gentlemen. With us or hightail it." He waved the gun around and the two cowboys took quick looks at each other and made for the door, just as Oakley had expected. "Don't be talking about this," he snarled at them. He looked at Willoughby and shook his head. "We don't got a lot of time, Mose." He tucked the gun away and made sure Willoughby was steady on his feet. "I'm thinking we ride into town and kidnap the banker, make him open that vault, take the money, and then blow up the bank and the banker with the dynamite."

"That's far better than what Hatfield had planned," Mose Willoughby said. "Starting to get some feelings back and some hearing back. Whew, but that does hurt."

"Get yourself put together. I'm gonna go check on the horses."

Lou Foster moved away from the side of the barn when the buckaroos left. Using brush and shadows, he moved quickly to his horse, got on, and walked the horse as quietly as he could out toward the road but Slim

Oakley saw him, yelled out, took a quick shot, and raced for his horse.

Foster was as low in the saddle as he could get, had his stock horse running wide open and raced through the night for Eureka, just a couple of miles distant. He had no trouble seeing as he got closer due to the bright light from the Eureka House conflagration. Oakley's horse wasn't up to the race, his shots went wild, and he seemed to give up after less than half a mile.

Foster passed the two buckaroos, yelling wildly at his horse, spurs dug in and raced to the Bonanza Club, figuring Oakley wouldn't dare follow him in. He didn't know no one was following him as he ran into the saloon.

CHAPTER NINE

CORCORAN WAS LAUGHING at what Sheriff Connor said and saw Lou Foster bound into the saloon. "Over here," he called out to the new deputy. "Looks like you might have found out something." The young former buckaroo had excitement written broad across his sweaty face as he came to their table.

"Found out I can ride a horse faster than Slim Oakley can," Foster said. He was breathing hard, and his eyes were lit up. "That's one hell of a fire out there."

"Oakley chased you? Better have a cold beer, catch your breath, and tell us all about it."

"It's pretty complicated, Corcoran, but here goes." He drained the glass and took a deep breath. "Willoughby killed Hank Sawyer. Oakley and Mose Willoughby are planning to blow up the bank. The two other men who were going to rob the bank ran off. The whole group was planning to rob the bank when it opens tomorrow morning. I'm pretty sure that plan has been changed. Willoughby had his ear shot off by Sawyer."

He got it all out in one long breath and grabbed for the beer mug. "Whew. Even got shot at," he said.

"You've been a busy boy," the sheriff laughed. "Better have another beer, son."

"Can't be robbing banks with just one ear, can you?" Corcoran couldn't hold in the guffaws, seeing this wild picture of a one-eared bandit. "Take your time, suck down another beer, and spill it out how they plan to rob the bank." He looked over to the sheriff. "Do you think either of those two yahoos know where banker Anderson lives? With that fire blazing and the town in an uproar, this would be the time to kidnap the old man and pull the robbery off."

"It would indeed," Connor said. "Know where he lives, Foster?"

"Isn't his house right behind the bank? The only brick house in town, I think."

"That's it. Hustle over there, wake Anderson up, and get him over to our office. I'll meet you there." Sheriff Connor was on his feet and Lou Foster was out the door. "You, my fine friend," he said to Corcoran, "need to be at that bank waiting for those two fools."

Corcoran had a smile on his face as he drained his beer. "Arson fire, two murders, and now a possible bank robbery. I love this sleepy little mining camp."

Foster left his horse tethered in front of the Bonanza Club and dog-trotted the two blocks down to the bank. It sat on a large corner lot with Anderson's impressive brick, two-story home facing the side street behind the bank. Foster ran up on the porch and banged on the front door, surprised that old man Anderson answered right away.

"I'm Deputy Sheriff Foster, sir. Sorry to waken you, but the sheriff wants you down at his office right away."

"The fire activity had me awake, son. What's the problem?" Anderson was near fifty, in excellent health and condition, tanned from spending more hours outside than in his hardwood paneled office, and unmarried despite the efforts of several lovely young ladies in Eureka.

"Sheriff fears a problem, possibly because of this fire. Please, come with me now," Foster said. He wasn't sure if he should say anything about the planned robbery but needed to have the banker understand the urgency of the matter. "Sheriff said the fire was intentionally set."

"Don't doubt it. Hatfield owes me plenty," Anderson said and walked out onto the porch pulling the door shut. "Let's go."

They walked back to the office through crowds of people continuing to flock to the fire. Foster had his eyes going over the crowd hoping that he would not spot either Willoughby or Oakley.

"If that fire gets away from them the whole town will go up," Anderson said. "Saw that in Virginia City last year. Whole damn town burned down. Had to blow up the church to stop it. Fire is a nasty business. Sheriff say he might think Hatfield started it? Wouldn't surprise me."

Foster didn't try to answer him, just kept pushing his way through the crowd. The noise of the fire crews, the blaze itself, and the yelling of the crowd was intense, and Foster was sure that at any moment one or both of the outlaws would come out of the crowd and grab the banker.

————

Corcoran took his time and slowly walked all the way around the Eureka Bank building, looking at possible points of entry. "The only way they'll get that vault open is to have a gun at Anderson's head," he mumbled. The back doors were locked solid and the only windows he could find were high up and none were open.

Corcoran left the bank and walked around to inspect the house. He stood near the walkway to Anderson's house letting his mind try to figure out how a robber would go about this. *Have to abduct the old man for sure. All right, we know that, what's Anderson's house like? One man living in a house that big,* he thought, looking at it. *Ain't my way of living.* The porch went three-quarters of the way around, there was a front door, and doorways on each of the sides of the building.

I could use two more people with me right now. There's a hundred ways of getting into that house. Corcoran walked around to the back of the brick-and-stone building and found yet another entranceway. *Damn. Make that three more people.* He had to chuckle as he tried the door, surprised to find it unlocked. *You don't suppose Willoughby and Oakley are already here?* Corcoran pulled his revolver and cocked it.

The door opened to a type of mud porch and the door into the house was locked tight. He let his breath out and walked back out into the night, slipping the gun back in its holster. He looked for where best to set up and wait for the outlaws.

———

SLIM OAKLEY and Mose Willoughby rode into the little mining camp and turned off the main street well before reaching the turmoil of the burning Eureka House. "We'll skirt around and come down toward the banker's place from above. That fire should keep most of the town nice and interested. You sure you're up to this?" Oakley asked.

Mose Willoughby didn't look like a man who was about to rob a bank. Blood was spattered all over his shirt and head, a bloody rag was tied around his head, and he wasn't really stable in the saddle. "I'll be fine," he snarled but Oakley had his doubts. "I'll have enough money to get two new ears if I want them," Willoughby tried to chuckle.

"What do you know about this banker? Anything? I don't know nothing about him other than his vault has a lot of money that wants to be in my pockets," Oakley said.

"He's a good hunter—he spends a lot of time outdoors and is a good rifle and shotgun shooter." Willoughby stopped and held his hand to his where his ear had been. He coughed and almost whimpered before continuing. The pain was obvious. "He lives alone, doesn't have any live-in help, so we won't run into extra guns. Don't know nothing about his house other than it's big."

Oakley gave his partner a long look, shaking his head. "I'm almost thinkin' we might call this off. Don't know nothing about his house, don't know how to get in, or where he might be inside. Don't know nothing about the bank or even if there really is a lot of money in there. And you ain't exactly fit for a fight right now."

"No, Slim, I'm fine. I want that money. We come all this way, give up our jobs to make this ride with Hatfield and Sawyer, and now it's just us. No. I want that money." Mose Willoughby knew he was hurting and also knew how much he wanted pockets full of someone else's money. "Ain't gonna chase cows the rest of my days, Slim," he laughed. "I'm gonna drink tequila and chase pretty women. I want that money."

Money has been a driver for many thousands of years, whether it was shells, pretty stones, gold, or sheets of paper—it could drive a man to extremes. Nations have fallen for its lack and men have been looked on as gods when their coffers were full. Mose Willoughby wanted full coffers, but was he physically able to fulfill his part of the job? Slim Oakley had his doubts but also wanted pockets full of coins of the realm.

"All right, then," Oakley said. "That's the house, down about a block and a half. The bank is right next to it. Best to tie off the horses and walk in slow and quiet. Let's come in from the back side, Mose. It'll be dark and we sure don't want to be seen."

"That fire's got everybody in town down there, Slim. This will be a Sunday walk in the sunshine, I think."

CHAPTER TEN

CORCORAN WALKED around the house one more time and decided that if he were going to try and break in, the back side would be best. *Bushes, trees, even some old farm equipment back there gives me some places to hide too. Course it gives them cover to come in through. Even if they hit from one of the sides, I'll be able to take them.* Corcoran was sure they wouldn't try to break in from the front. Too much of a chance of being seen.

To make this work the two outlaws had to be quiet on the one hand and unseen as well. They would have to snare old man Anderson and force him into the bank, force him to open the vault, tie him up, and then fill sacks with as much money as they would hold, set the dynamite, and leave. They would have to skirt their way around the crowds to get out of town. Both Oakley and Willoughby knew the odds were against them from the start. It was the prize that made the effort worthwhile.

Corcoran crouched behind a stand of brush and spotted shadows up the street moving slowly toward the

Anderson home. The two men were on the west side of the north-south street, staying in the shadows as much as they could, each carrying a rifle and sacks filled with something. It was dynamite but Corcoran couldn't know that.

That one boy ain't too steady on his feet, Corcoran said to himself watching the two. *Wonder if he's missing an ear?* He had a hard time holding in a snicker. They were much closer than they looked at first. Corcoran eased his rifle up to his shoulder. Slim stepped off the street, parted a scrubby hedge and slipped into the banker's backyard, less than twenty feet from Corcoran.

When Willoughby followed, Corcoran stood up. "Far enough, boys. Drop the guns." There was enough light from the raging fire a few blocks to the east that he and his rifle were well lit. Oakley pulled the shotgun up but was far too slow and took a bullet through his chest for the effort. Willoughby on the other hand decided the best offense was to run as fast as his wobbly legs would go.

Corcoran sprinted after the wounded buckaroo and slammed his rifle across the back of the outlaw's head when he quickly caught up. Mose Willoughby went face down on the gravel street and didn't move. A rifle blast in a neighborhood would generally bring lots of people out, but with one of the town's large hotel-saloons on fire, there was no one to come out. *Shame no one saw that. It was a perfect nose-first dive.* Corcoran laughed at his thought, trying to get Willoughby on his feet.

He walked the woozy man back to Anderson's place in time to meet Lou Foster who had run back when he heard the gunshot. "Oakley's body is on the other side of the hedge, Lou," Corcoran said. "Better run and bring the doc back. Tell him he'll need the wagon. I'll get this yahoo over to the jail. After he sends the body off, he'll need to come to the jail and take care of this fool."

"Might want to hurry, Terrence. Anderson isn't happy about being brought in to the sheriff. Sheriff's having a hard time convincing him that he was going to be abducted."

———

BANKER ANDERSON WAS SITTING across the desk from Sheriff Connor when Corcoran brought Mose Willoughby in. "This is why I brought you down here, Anderson," Connor said. "Just one, Corcoran?"

"No, Ed, Slim Oakley died in the attempt." Corcoran looked at Anderson and pushed Willoughby across the room to another chair. "Sit," he growled, forcing the man down. "Foster was right, Ed. Man's only got one ear."

"You cut off his ear?" Anderson asked, jumping to his feet. "That's horrible. That man needs a doctor."

"I did not," Corcoran said, "and the doc will be here shortly. Banker Anderson, meet Mose Willoughby. He and his late partner, Slim Oakley, were going to kidnap you and make you open the vault at your bank. As you can see, that isn't gonna happen." Corcoran shook his head, wanting to say considerably more but let it go. "If you'll excuse me, I'll get this fool booked into our fine hotel."

Corcoran grabbed some papers off Connor's desk, got

Willoughby up, and shoved him through the door to where the cells were. "Send the doc back when he gets here. Any more on the fire?"

"Arson for sure, Terrence. Found one of Hatfield's faro dealer's body along with two cans that had kerosene in them at one time. Hatfield's vault was open and empty, so considerable amounts of money are currently unaccounted for. Did he have any with him when he died?"

"Maybe fifty bucks, sheriff. Somebody got there. We'll need to get all his employees together as this calms down. Fun little town, eh Mr. Anderson?" He closed and locked the door behind him escorting his prisoner.

"WELL, Anderson, now you know some of the story," Sheriff Connor said. "Hank Sawyer shot Willoughby's ear off, not Corcoran. He and Oakley were in your backyard to kidnap you and rob your bank. Right now, just so you know, we're investigating the murder of Maria Castelleno, the murder of Gordon Hatfield, the arson fire that is destroying the Eureka House, and now, your attempted kidnapping and robbery of the Eureka Bank. Apologies are not necessary as you leave for home."

Banker Anderson harrumphed twice as he hustled out the door, almost knocking Doctor Whidby aside. "Come right in, Doc. Got a live one for you. Lou, knock on the door and get Doctor Whidby in to see our one-eared bandit. Keeping you busy, eh?"

"Too damn busy, Ed. How many more?"

Lou Foster looked at Ed Connor then the doctor. "Anyone tell him about what's out at that barn?"

"Damn," Connor said. "We got to get out there, Lou. There's supposed to be dynamite and several stolen rifles."

"Along with Hank Sawyer's body," Foster said. "Think the dynamite is with Oakley's body."

Doc Whidby said, "Yeah. Dynamite, caps, and fuse. You can pick it up at my place on your way out." He stood next to the cell area door and cussed for one full minute before Lou could get Corcoran to unlock the door. Foster motioned for Corcoran to stay with the sheriff and he would take the doc to Mose Willoughby. "Might want to calm the sheriff down some. I'll try to calm the doc."

Corcoran chuckled walking to the stove to pour a cup of coffee. "We're gonna take a long, slow ride out to Hatfield's barn, Corcoran," Sheriff Connor almost snarled, "and you're going to tell me how we're going to solve Maria Castelleno's murder. Then you'll tell me how we're gonna solve Gordon Hatfield's murder. Got that?"

"Clear as the sunrise tomorrow morning, sheriff. The only thing we know for sure is that Willoughby killed Sawyer and the rest of the deaths are probably not connected."

"I don't know about that, Terrence." Connor sat back in his chair. "Isn't it possible that Castelleno killed both Maria and Hatfield?"

"Oh, hell yes. I meant not connected to Sawyer's death. Foster said he heard Sawyer say it was Hatfield's plan to rob the bank but it was Willoughby and Oakley who were actually doing it. Any of several people could have killed Hatfield and, damn it, any of half a dozen people could have killed Maria. Let's take that ride, sheriff. It's a murder scene so we don't need to check with the judge first.

———————

"I was sure that Pete Ainsley told us there were half a dozen rifles taken in that robbery at Gensler's Gun Store. We've got nine guns here and there were only going to be five men involved in the robbery. Six if you include Hatfield." Sheriff Ed Connor was standing in the middle of the large barn looking at the stack of rifles.

"Got half a case of dynamite, blasting caps, and fuse over here," Corcoran said. "If Hatfield's plan was to kidnap Anderson, make him open the vault and then blow up the bank after they emptied it, they would have been over supplied, sheriff. More guns than people and more explosives than anyone would need. Too much planning by people who can't plan."

"Well, let's get this stuff loaded in that wagon out there, get Sawyer's body in, too, and take it all back to town. We'll get Foster to round up the Eureka House employees, come morning, and see what we can find out."

"Might let you and him talk to them, sheriff. I need to talk with Castelleno. I let him get away with the unconscious stuff but won't do that again. With Hatfield dead, Maria dead, and somebody paid somebody to burn down the hotel, he's my only suspect. I'm going to catch some sleep in the spare cell and head out there early."

"Get back as quick as you can. With all this turmoil, sure as hell one or more of our rowdies will try to rob or kill thinking we're too wrapped up in this other crap," the sheriff said.

CHAPTER ELEVEN

It wasn't a long ride from town to the Castelleno Mine, but it gave Corcoran plenty of time to do some serious thinking. *Somebody burned down the Eureka House, but did they do that on Hatfield's orders? Or did they have a grudge of their own? Or, and this is more likely, did they burn the place down on Alphonso Castelleno's orders? Taking that another step or two, did Castelleno murder Maria or hire it done? Did Castelleno murder Hatfield or hire it done?*

In his long career as a lawman, Corcoran was well aware of the fact that sometimes he jumped to the wrong conclusions, but overall, in his estimation, his first impressions were right more often than not. On the other hand, he had to admit to himself, it was he who shot the sheriff whom he worked for. The thought brought a quick chuckle to the large man.

"I got my work cut out, eh Dude?" he called out to his horse. "Now listen for a minute, old man. What if it wasn't Castelleno? Who else had a reason to kill Maria? To kill Hatfield? To demolish the hotel?" He rode in silence for a while letting all the questions roam around in his mind and coming up with no answers of any kind.

"All right, Dude, we'll have to do this the hard way, I guess." He rode into the mine owner's homeplace and tied off at the hitching post. It was a short walk up a narrow pathway to the house. A young Mexican boy answered the door when Corcoran pounded.

"Name's Corcoran, Terrence Corcoran, here to see Castelleno," he said to the boy. The boy shook his head and started to shut the door but Corcoran shoved the door open, pushed the boy aside, and walked into the great room. Castelleno was standing with his back to the fireplace.

"What the hell is this?" Castelleno demanded. "How dare you?"

"Good morning," Corcoran said. "Good to see you're feeling better. We have a few things to discuss, sir."

"You're not welcome here," Castelleno said. "You were not invited into my home. You must leave."

"Or what, Castelleno? No, I'm not leaving," Corcoran said. He was wrong, knew he was wrong, but was going to have this discussion no matter what. He had a smile on his face, but Castelleno could see no smile in his eyes. "I'm here and here I'll stay until we have our little talk. Shall we sit and talk like gentlemen?" He waited just a moment and continued. "Or would you rather I bring you to the sheriff's office for our chat?"

Castelleno was boxed in and he knew it. He was a dignified southern European gentleman, would not want to be seen escorted into the jail facility, and would not want his people at the mine talking about their patron being led out by this peon of a deputy.

"Please, Deputy Corcoran, sit," Castelleno said, quietly. The gentleman looked at the young boy. "Pedro, bring us coffee, por favor. And a bottle of brandy." He looked at Corcoran, walked to a large, overstuffed chair and took his seat. Corcoran sat in its twin, across from Castelleno. "Now, what should we discuss?"

"We have a full agenda, I'm afraid. Your wife Maria's murder, Gordon Hatfield's murder, and the torching of the Eureka House. The last time we spoke, you might remember, you were on a mission to kill Gordon Hatfield. Shall we start with where you were on the morning Maria was murdered?"

Castelleno had a horribly pained expression on his face and slumped back in the chair. "Ah, Maria. She was so exciting, so alive, and gone just like that. She wasn't the best wife a man could have, I'm sure you understand." He wagged his head back and forth, sad eyes probing Corcoran's. "She craved excitement. Some of the men, men like Hatfield, took advantage of those cravings. I couldn't blame Maria, but those men, I blame." Hurt from the loss of his wife to hatred for the men involved flushed his face.

Corcoran looked at the man and knew he would never understand that kind of thinking. His wife is flirting with any man she runs across, has had affairs with so many, Hatfield, in particular, and was planning a picnic with someone. *He says he can't blame Maria but does blame the men. What about Rosita? Why did he beat on her but doesn't blame Maria?*

"All that is fine, sir," Corcoran said, "but where were you that morning?"

"I was here at home until around nine and then went to the mine. I watched Rosita and Maria drive off, knew there would be men later, and was very angry. I needed to work my anger off. I went to the mine and joined with one of the crews for some heavy work. There are half a dozen men will testify to that."

He watched Maria and Rosita drive off and knew there would be men involved? Men? Did he believe that Maria and Rosita were going to entertain men? Was Rosita a procurer?

"You knew Maria would be meeting with men and yet you didn't try to stop her? Why?"

"She never actually did anything other than tease these men," Castelleno said. "You see, Deputy Corcoran, she had to have her excitement, had to feel wanted. She craved it, sir."

"And yet, you were drunk and looking to kill Gordon Hatfield just the other day and knew there was far more than teasing going on." Corcoran wasn't able to understand the man's thinking. "It's all right for her to meet with some man for a picnic but you were ready to kill Hatfield for what? For what?" he said again.

Castelleno was still slumped back in his chair when Pedro came back in. He had a tray with a coffee urn and cups, and a bottle of Italian brandy. The boy poured the coffee cups almost full and produced small snifters for the brandy, bowed slightly to Castelleno, frowned at Corcoran, and left the room.

"He's a good boy, Pedro is. My sister's. She is married

to a Spanish miner in Peru and wanted the boy to learn our ways, that is, American ways. My sister and her husband were killed in some kind of uproar, and he's been with us for almost two years now. My only heir, Corcoran."

"You and Maria had no children?"

"Such a shame. Children from that wonderful and wild woman would have been so beautiful. No, my Maria was unable to have children. She loved Pedro." Castelleno tried his best to smile and failed.

"You were very angry at Rosita Chavez the other morning, hit her, which is something a gentleman should never do, and fired the lady." *He's a contradiction, says one thing and does another. It's all right for Maria to meet some man for a picnic but not meet Hatfield for a supper. It's all right for Maria to plan a picnic but not all right for Rosita to help her with it. Does he love Maria or is he in love with his idea of who Maria should be?*

"Sir," Corcoran said, after a taste of the delicious brandy, "what is the difference between Maria having a picnic with some man but not all right with her having supper with Gordon Hatfield?"

Castelleno looked at Corcoran almost quizzically. "I'm afraid a man of your sort simply wouldn't understand," he said.

My sort? Why hasn't this man asked me how my investigation is going? He has evaded every single question I've asked yet says he was at the mine, has men who will verify he was at the mine. Corcoran gave a studied look at Castelleno.

"My sort, sir, is to find the killer of Maria and to do that, I ask questions. You haven't answered the questions.

Why were you looking to kill Gordon Hatfield the other day?"

For the first time since arriving, Corcoran could see anger in the man's face. Anger was replacing generations of arrogance. "Hatfield took advantage of Maria's teasing." He snarled it out and sat straight up in his chair. "The man is dead? Good. I will tell you now, I did not kill my wife. I did not kill that swine, Hatfield. You can check with any of my men. I have been here on the mine property from the morning of Maria's death until this moment."

"Then sir, tell me why you were angry enough to hit and then fire Rosita Chavez?"

"Ah, Rosita. Such a wounded little animal she is. Suffered greatly as a child, humiliated by a whore for a mother and a bandit for a father. She never attended school for a day, was treated as a slave by those who took her in, by those who used her." He sat back in the chair, looked up at the ceiling and then to the fire.

"It was my beloved Maria who brought Rosita into our lives—a spoiled, bruised, and rotten child, living on the streets, peddling herself to whoever would buy. She had no morals, knew not wrong from right, but thrived with Maria's love and a full plate three times a day."

He took a long breath, another sip of the excellent brandy, and continued. "Rosita became a part of our family overnight and was Maria's shadow. I wasn't angry at Rosita, I never touched the woman, and certainly didn't fire her. She had a terrible habit of hurting herself, banging her head against the wall, and using heavy wood to hit herself.

"No, Deputy Corcoran, I didn't hit the child and didn't fire her. She hit herself, took my horse and buggy, and left. I'm almost certain that she will return."

What a strange household this must have been. It will take me three days to try and understand all of what Castelleno has said today. Corcoran finished the brandy, stood up, told Castelleno he would probably be back with more questions, and left the building. *I don't know why but I believe the man. He lives by strange ways, but I don't think he was lying to me. That is not to say he didn't arrange for the deaths of Maria and Hatfield. That, I think will be my focus now. I wonder if I might learn something more about the man if I talk with Rosita.*

CHAPTER TWELVE

LOU FOSTER ROUNDED up most of the employees of the Eureka House and had them at a table in a conference room at the courthouse. The sheriff's office was just too small for such a meeting. Ed Connor looked over the tired and grubby bunch who had spent a great amount of time working to help put out the fire.

"Thank you for coming," Connor said. "This is a nasty business and I'll try to get it over with as quickly as possible. I'll call out a name and please answer." He looked over to Foster who slowly read off six names. Only five answered that they were there. Steve Knight, one of the men who worked the faro tables was missing.

"Mr. Knight was the man who was found dead," Tony Soma answered and Connor nodded. Soma started to say something else, but Connor cut him off. Knight's body had been found with the cans of kerosene, but Connor didn't know how much of that information was known by those at the table.

"We'll start with you, Tony. What exactly took place

just as the fire erupted? Was Gordon Hatfield in the building?"

Tony Soma was the long-standing barman at the Eureka House, had been there with the previous owner as well. "It was a busy morning, sheriff. Hatfield had some men in for some kind of meeting and they were waiting for Hank Sawyer. It was some time before he arrived and there was lots of drinking during that time. When Sawyer finally led the men out, Hatfield went upstairs for a while, and then came down and left the building. The fire broke out just a few minutes after he left."

"Where did it break out?" Connor asked. "Was it upstairs? Where Hatfield had been?" That brought general comments from many in the room and Connor shushed them with a stern look.

"No," Soma said. "No, the fire broke out in the back storage room. Where a lot of the liquor is stored. It was a fast fire, sheriff, and hot as hell. I can still feel it."

Connor looked around at the gathering. "Anybody disagree with that?" No one spoke up and Connor continued. "Tony, do you know what the meeting was about? Anybody say anything that seemed unusual?"

"There was talk of new rifles, but no one said why Hatfield would be giving them rifles. Willoughby and Oakley were off by themselves in some kind of serious discussion." Soma hesitated for a moment and shook his head. "I never heard, I guess what the meeting was about. Sawyer was late showing up, Hatfield didn't seem to care but the others were tense when he did walk in."

"We're sure it was Mr. Knight who started the fire. His body was found with empty kerosene cans. Doctor

Whidby says he was shot before his body was consumed by the flames." That was not generally known, and Connor waited for some kind of reaction. He didn't get much other than raised eyebrows. "Is it at all possible for Hatfield to get from his upstairs office down to that storeroom without being seen in the saloon?"

"Sure," Tony Soma answered. "The office has a doorway onto the second floor of the hotel and the hotel has its own entrance into the downstairs storeroom. Hatfield went back and forth between the saloon and hotel regularly."

"I wonder why no one heard the gunshot?" Lou Foster said, looking around the group. He saw Tony Soma take a quick look at a man called Atkins. George Atkins. Connor picked up on that as well and Atkins squirmed around some in his chair. Was he going to run? Foster moved over toward the doorway.

"Thank you all for coming." Connor said. "It's going to be difficult for some of you and the county will do what it can to help in some way. Mr. Atkins, I wonder if you'll stay for just a minute or two."

Atkins showed definite signs of not wanting to stay but knew that Lou Foster was at the doorway, and he could not fight that large man. Atkins, a faro dealer like Knight, was tall and thin, not known for doing any kind of physical work. As with most of the gamblers working tables on the frontier, Atkins carried a small gun. Some had them up their sleeves, some in their boots, but most had one or two close at hand.

Atkins sat back down as the others filed out and Foster shut the door and joined Connor at the table. He stood directly behind the gambler. "Mr. Atkins would you be kind enough to ease that little pistol from your coat sleeve? Nice and slow, now." Atkins felt the barrel of Foster's revolver pressed against the back of his head and did as he was asked, setting the single-shot Derringer-type weapon on the table.

"Thank you," Connor said. He picked the gun up and broke it open, finding one empty casing in the receiver. He slipped the empty out and set it down. "These things usually make a loud blast for such a small weapon. How did you muffle the sound, Mr. Atkins?"

Atkins sat quiet and didn't say a word. "Mr. Hatfield came down into the storeroom and met with Mr. Knight, gave him considerable money, went back upstairs and then left the building in front of everyone. You knew what had happened didn't you? You and Knight knew the plan, didn't you?"

Connor had had Atkins in his jail before—petty larceny, accused of cheating at the table, even one of attempted robbery at the mercantile store. Connor knew that Atkins bought the kerosene that Knight used to burn down the hotel-saloon complex. By accident, Burt Kinder mentioned it when discussing the fire with the sheriff.

Atkins sat in silence and Connor continued. Connor was working on his own conjecture, didn't have anything but the sale of kerosene and that quick look from Soma to go on. "Hatfield paid Knight to burn the building in order to get the insurance and you knew it because you and Knight were supposed to be partners in the plan. You slipped into the storage room, muffled that little shooter, and killed Knight. After you emptied his pockets of the gold that Hatfield had just brought him, you poured the last of the kerosene all over him and lit the fire off. What did you use, a wadded-up rag to muffle the shot?"

"You don't know what you're talking about. I was at my table when the fire started. I didn't kill nobody."

"More than one person will testify that you weren't at your table, sir. You see, we know Hatfield emptied his vault before he left the building. We also know that when we found his body, he only had a small amount of cash with him." With a satisfied look on his face, Connor picked up the little gun and stood up. "Knight brought you into the game, you bought the kerosene, helped him spread gallons of it around the building, and then killed your partner and took the gold." He looked over to Foster.

"Better put the cuffs on this gentleman, Mr. Foster. Let's take him to jail, shall we? And then we'll take a little walk to his cabin and search for that gold."

They had no trouble finding the gold as Atkins had it bundled tightly in wooden boxes ready for transport out of town. "Again, Mr. Foster, welcome to our fine little department. Your catching the look from Tony Soma gave us all of this."

CHAPTER THIRTEEN

CORCORAN FOUND Jimmy Henderson behind the bar at his own saloon and motioned for a cold beer. "Grass'll grow with this kind of heat, Jimmy. Them cows'll get fat and tasty this spring."

"You're in good spirits, Terrence. Any idea on who killed Maria Castelleno? Besides the burnt-out Eureka House, that's the only other thing people are talking about."

"That's why I'm here," Corcoran said. "Is Rosita in? I just left Castelleno and need to have a chat with her."

"I think you'll find her in the kitchen, Terrence. She is a good cook and Cindy hired her on. The girl was destitute. That old bastard didn't just beat her and fire her, he sent her off without a dime. The man has a cruel streak, Terrence. A bad one."

Corcoran cocked his head to the side, thinking about that. *More questions about Castelleno. Was he lying to me about Rosita? He said she regularly hurt herself. She shows up bruised and broke. I need answers and soon.*

"Well, Jimmy, he also had a wife with a wandering eye. I just left the man and I'm thoroughly confused by his reaction to all this." He didn't go any further with the thought knowing that whatever he said would be spread through town in minutes.

Corcoran was about to finish his beer when Cindy Cook came racing across the floor of the saloon and flung herself into his arms. "Terrence," she almost moaned, wrapping her arms around the big man. "You promised to come over last night. I was so lonely."

"Maybe you didn't notice, but the town almost burned down last night," he laughed. He wrapped his arms around the tiny girl, squeezed her tight and sat her down in his lap. "If I promise to come over tonight, barring any more conflagrations or murders, can I have a long talk with your new cook?"

"Rosita's not your kind, Terrence. I'm your kind." She giggled and tried to steal a kiss but Corcoran saw it coming and tucked his head. "Question me, Terrence. I'll tell you everything I know. Even more if you want."

He stood up and set the girl down. "Unfortunately, dear girl, this is business. How's Rosita holding up? Any problems?"

"She's carrying a great hate for Mr. Castelleno. She says she and Maria were not very close and is sure Castelleno is the one who killed Maria."

"Thank you. See you tonight." He started to make his way toward the kitchen when Ed Connor walked in and motioned for him to join him at a table. "Better get us a couple of cold ones, Jimmy. He's got that look on his face."

"Got a couple of things cleared up," the sheriff said as Corcoran took his seat. "George Atkins killed Knight and actually started the fire at the Eureka House. He and Knight were partners, it seems. Hatfield paid Knight to burn the place in order to collect the insurance and Atkins killed Knight to claim all the gold."

"That's good news but we still don't know who killed Hatfield. I wonder how much of all this is connected? The fire, the two murders, and the attempted bank robbery? I just got back from talking with Castelleno and am more confused than when I left this morning." Corcoran started to say that he was of the opinion that Castelleno was not involved in Maria's murder but changed his mind.

"I was about to have a talk with Rosita Chavez. Care to join me?"

"No. Lou Foster and I are going to interview Willoughby again. Doc Whidby says the man will live to see prison. Then we're going to ransack Atkins's cabin."

———

CORCORAN FOUND Rosita Chavez at the woodstove in the Bonanza Club's kitchen, stirring a large pot of bean soup. "That smells so good I could eat the whole pot, Rosita," he said. "How about we sit at the table with some coffee and have a little chat."

She frowned but grabbed the hefty coffee pot and came to the table. Corcoran had cups ready. "Can't leave that soup for very long," she said. The scratches on her face were healing, the bruises weren't quite as obvious, but Rosita wasn't the bubbly and friendly woman she had been.

"I just left Castelleno, Rosita. He seems to think you and Maria were going to meet some men at that picnic. Is that the case?"

"No!" Rosita spat it out. "It was Maria who was meeting someone. No. I don't meet men for picnics." She was leaning forward in the chair, glaring at the deputy, daring him to accuse her of such a thing. "It was Castelleno who made me go with her, to keep her from doing something wrong. Something bad."

She doesn't meet men for picnics? She's very attractive yet there's been no mention of a man in her life. Her tone of voice says she and Maria were not best of friends either.

"I thought you and Maria were best of friends?" Corcoran hadn't heard any of this before and it changed several of his thoughts. "So why did Castelleno beat you when you got back?"

"Because Maria was dead. He blamed me for not protecting her. She did these horrible things with men, things married women don't do, and I was supposed to protect her."

Corcoran sat still for a minute letting this soak in. *Castelleno says it's the men who are wrong but sends Rosita to protect his wife? The man needs a good beating himself. Married to a woman who does not sanctify marriage but blames the men then beats his housemaid for not protecting her? That's Rosita's story and just the opposite of the old man's story. Who to believe?*

"Rosita, has this happened before? Has he beat you for not protecting Maria before?" Corcoran saw that the lady was looking straight into his eyes when she answered.

"Yes." She got up and walked to the stove to stir the bean soup. She gave it a sound stirring. "More than once," she murmured.

"Will you give me the names of the men Maria has had picnics with? Men she has had suppers with? Men she may have been with that led to your getting a beating from Castelleno?" His voice was soft and quiet as he asked. Had Rosita been used by the old man, used in such a way that if she didn't intervene in Maria's activities, she would be blamed for the indiscretion, not Maria? *Castelleno has his values upside down and Rosita gets the bruises.*

"I don't know who the men were," she said. "The only man I know was Mr. Hatfield because he had Maria up to his room for their suppers. I never saw any of the men at the picnics."

"You weren't involved? How is that?" Corcoran asked.

"I was to stay with the horse and wagon, Corcoran. I wasn't to be with Maria. It's so terrible. It was so wrong and if I didn't do what I was told, Maria would not pay me. No matter what I did, I got hurt in some way." The anger flashed in her brown eyes, her normally warm smile was well hidden, and Corcoran's thoughts gave ample reason for murder.

"Thank you," Corcoran said and walked out of the kitchen and back to the office. *Is what I'm hearing from Castelleno the European way of handling wayward women in marriage or is it Castelleno's way? Or, has what Rosita just told me a total lie? The laws being broken are Maria's murder and Castelleno's beating of Rosita so I've got to put aside Castelleno's strange ways and concentrate on solving the murder. My personal feelings have no place in this investigation. But I still want to beat the hell out of that man. I may yet get that opportunity.*

———

"So, Terrence, did you and Rosita have your meeting? She's a very pretty girl, you know." Cindy Cook had a concerned look on her face as she snuggled under the covers with Corcoran. "She really hates both Maria and old man Castelleno."

Solving a murder was not the reason for this visit and was not foremost in Terrence Corcoran's mind at the moment, but Cindy's comments put it there immediately. "There are many other things we need to discuss and enjoy this lovely evening, Miss Cindy Cook," he chuckled. He kissed her neck and let his hands rove about some. "But I do want to ask you a big favor."

"There is nothing I won't do for you, big man. You know that. Let's not be getting into something serious and ruin this night."

"Just for a minute or two. All I'm asking is that you let me know anything you and Rosita talk about." He was sure Rosita knew more about Maria's death than she had told him. Rosita said she saw the man with the rock kill her but also said that she never knew any of the men Maria had these little affairs with—that she was banned from being a part of the program. *If that's the case then how is it that she saw the man with the rock? She knows more than she's saying.*

"Does Rosita have any man friends? Anyone that might be special?"

"You mean special like us?" She teased. "I don't know but I'll tell you if I find out," she whispered. Cindy cuddled up as close to Corcoran as she could get and promised to tell him everything she and Rosita talked about. "Everything, big boy." The rest of the evening was active, even somewhat noisy from time to time.

———————

"Where are you off to this early in the morning, Corcoran?" Foster had the stove lit and coffee boiling before Corcoran arrived. "Sheriff is over at the Bonanza having breakfast. Said to tell you to join him."

"That's a good idea, Lou. I could eat a whole bear this morning. Our prisoners taken care of?"

"Had their bowls of boiled oats and coffee. Willoughby's feeling sickly and Atkins ain't talking. Everything's fine back there."

"Good," Corcoran chuckled. "Add some wood to the fire and let's join the sheriff for breakfast. Willoughby talk about anything?"

"Said he's gonna kill all of us when he gets out of here. He's done some scratching around the base of the windows in the cell and seems to think he can break out."

"He won't," Corcoran snarled. "Can't seem to figure out who it was who shot Gordon Hatfield. Or why. Lots of people had nasty thoughts about the man, but murder? That's as nasty as you can get. I was hoping our Mr. Willoughby might mention something."

"I'll work on that," Foster said.

It was a short walk up the street to the Bonanza Club and they found Sheriff Connor at the bar instead of the café. He had coffee and a bottle and was talking with the district attorney. "Ah, Terrence, Lou, glad you made it." He turned to DA Phelps. "Let's take a table, shall we Bill? I've ordered steaks and eggs all the way around."

"You're in a generous mood this morning, Ed," Corcoran chuckled. "What brought all this on?" They found a big round table near one of the windows that looked out on the broad main street of Eureka and settled in. Rosita brought coffee and a basket of hot biscuits. She had freshly churned butter and blackberry jam on the table for them as well.

Connor looked at Phelps and nodded. "The district attorney has some information that might help our investigations out some. Go ahead, Bill. Repeat for them what you told me."

"Mr. Hatfield took the train to Reno last month and bought a rather large insurance policy on the Eureka House complex. To the tune of one hundred thousand dollars in the event of fire. This nasty business was planned some time ago. The insurance men will be in town on tomorrow's train."

"They surely can't be planning to pay it off," Corcoran said. "My god, man, we have enough evidence of arson to convict anyone twice over."

"These boys are from San Francisco and consider us country bumpkins, I'm afraid. They will be demanding." Phelps was impressed with anyone who claimed to be from San Francisco. The city was there for those at the pinnacle of their careers.

"They can be as demanding as they want," Connor said. "I'll let 'em sit on the kerosene cans while they demand." Connor laughed at his own comment and looked at Corcoran. "Anything to report on Mrs. Castelleno's murder?"

"Going out to the mine again this morning, Ed. Castelleno talks in riddles but so far doesn't appear to have lied to me. He's implicated in Maria's death and has to be considered a suspect in Hatfield's death. He hated that man."

Connor looked over to the district attorney, asking with his eyes to say something but Phelps went out of his way not to make eye contact. Corcoran caught all of the sly movements and knew that he and Connor would have something to talk about when they were alone. Not now. "Were you able to recover any of the gold that Hatfield paid Knight and Atkins?" Corcoran asked instead.

"There was a total of five hundred dollars in gold and bills at the cabin," Connor said.

"That's what Hatfield had promised the two," Lou Foster said. "Mose Willoughby laughed when Atkins told me. Called Hatfield a cheap sumbitch."

"I wonder what his cut was going to be after the bank robbery?" Connor asked. "Do you suppose Willoughby killed Hatfield?"

"No, he rode out with Hank Sawyer and the others, but I remember Tony Soma saying that Slim Oakley almost followed Hatfield out of the saloon. He wasn't with the gang at the barn. Showed up later. After the fire started," Lou Foster said.

"You're onto something, there, Lou," Corcoran said. "How about you have a talk with that lawyer, Ed Graves. He was first on the scene of Hatfield's murder. Maybe you can get him to remember something."

Breakfast took another full hour of pleasantries and finally broke up. "I'll bring those insurance men to your office, Ed, as soon as they arrive," Phelps said.

"Yeah, you do that," Connors growled. "Try to be there, Corcoran, so I don't shoot one of 'em. You, too, Foster. Country bumpkins my ass."

Corcoran chuckled watching Phelps make his way out of the restaurant. "There something you want to tell me about Phelps? He's easily impressed by people in high places."

"His wife more so," Connor said. "I'm not sure about this, Corcoran, but I would check on Phelps's doings when his wife is out of town. He may know more about Maria Castelleno than either of us."

CHAPTER FOURTEEN

"Good morning, Mr. Castelleno. Have a couple more questions I need to discuss with you." Corcoran relished the ride out to the mine following that large breakfast. *A couple of those biscuits would have been more than enough for me. I was hungry as hell until I started eating. Must have been the company. Something going on between the sheriff and the DA.*

"What now, deputy?" Castelleno said. Corcoran didn't wait to be invited in but stepped into the large living room, slightly brushing Castelleno.

"Spent some time with Rosita Chavez and," he paused, glaring at the elderly man. "Well, sir, it isn't a gentleman's way to beat on one's hired help. Tell me about this. You told Rosita to go with your wife on these trysts and then slapped her around if she didn't try to stop whatever was taking place?"

"Maria couldn't help herself, as I've told you. It was Rosita's duty to help her. To keep her from...from..." and he broke down, almost losing his balance. Was it anger?

Or grief? Corcoran couldn't tell as he stepped forward, took the man by his shoulders, and got him into one of the large chairs near the fireplace.

The biggest fool I've ever met. Willing to beat a woman who worked for him and willing to let his wife have her flings because she couldn't help herself. And hating everyone around him because he is the weak one here. Did he kill her? I'm saying no for the time being. Did he have her killed? That question is open. He is capable of hiring it done but was he willing?

"Did you know that Rosita and your wife did not get along? Were not friendly with each other?"

"That's not true. And, another thing. I told you I never laid a hand on Rosita. She's lying to you, deputy. Maria loved Rosita like a daughter, and Rosita worshipped my Maria and would do anything for her, but was weak, wouldn't stop her from doing terrible things."

Corcoran looked down on the man. Castelleno was weeping, almost curling up in the overstuffed chair and Corcoran shook his head, turned, and walked out of the house. "You'll be hearing from me," he said. The ride back to town was slow as Corcoran tried to understand the relationship Alphonso must have had with Maria.

Relationship. There's an interesting word in this instance. I wonder how Maria would have explained their relationship. His explanation is one as weird as I ever want to hear about. None of this has gotten me one bit closer to who killed Maria Castelleno. After Castelleno, Mr. Hatfield is number one suspect, but I must not forget how angry Abe Afeldt was. He has a good alibi, but he stays in the game. George Florencio was known to have been teased by Maria as well.

Corcoran all at once pulled Dude up short. "Rosita,"

he murmured. *Rosita did not get along with Maria because of how she treated her marriage, but what about the old man? Did he have this desire for the wild life as well? Is his relationship with Rosita foul because she turned his advances down? She's a very attractive woman. That's good, Terrence. Now you've added another wrinkle to the game.* He was chuckling softly as he nudged Dude into a healthy trot.

He says he never hit her and says she hurts herself. I wonder if they have had some kind of relationship? He had to chuckle thinking that if he kept it up, he would have half the population of Eureka as suspects in the woman's death.

CORCORAN PUT Dude up in the courthouse stables and took a short walk down into the gulch along the north edge of town, lined with houses, cabins, and in some cases, shacks. It was a small house surrounded by natural vegetation such as sage, rabbit brush, and stunted cedar —no fencing and only a mud track leading to the front door.

"Good morning, Tony," Corcoran said. "Got time for a couple of questions?"

Tony Soma opened the door wide. "Corcoran, well, come in. I just put a pot of coffee on. Wouldn't be here to offer me a job, would you?"

"Oh, well, no, I'm afraid not. Have you talked with Jimmy Henderson? You do have a good reputation around town. No, I'm here to talk about Gordon Hatfield, if you have the time." He took a seat at a table that served as kitchen table, living room table, and nightstand in the two-room cabin. "Other than the men who were with him the day of the fire, what other contacts did Hatfield have? Who would be considered fairly close to the man?"

"Not many, Corcoran. He was difficult to get along with on his best days. He had a hard time welcoming people to the operation." Soma laughed a little as he brought the coffee pot to the table. "He didn't look on people as customers, instead, they were to be picked clean. None of the games were honest, the liquor was cut considerably."

He poured the coffee and looked up at the ceiling for a moment or two, thinking. "None of the county people came in, not like the Bonanza Club, except for one. Bill Phelps seemed to be able to get along with Hatfield. Of course, they had one thing in common."

"Oh?" Corcoran stiffened at the comment. "Something in common between our district attorney and Hatfield? Go on, Tony, please."

"Well, Mrs. Castelleno of course. Hatfield had her up to his offices for supper more than once, and from what I was able to glean, as Phelps and Hatfield talked, the attorney hosted her at his place as well. They would mention something and both would break out in laughter, nodding in agreement at whatever was said."

"Most amazing," Corcoran said. Did Connor know this? Why hadn't he said something? This changed Corcoran's list of possible suspects dramatically. "I was under the impression that Mr. Phelps was married."

"I think in name only. His wife spends more time in Virginia City and San Francisco than she does in Eureka,"

Soma said. "She's never set foot in either the Eureka House Restaurant or the Bonanza Club café. Not good enough for her. She's a very cold woman."

"One thing I've learned in all these years of wearing a badge, Tony, is if you want to know about what's going on, ask your favorite bartender. Thank you for all that. Were you at all friendly with Knight or Atkins? It's a nasty business burning out a man's business, even if that man paid you to do it."

"Knight was the nicer of the two, but Atkins had eyes for the women. He always saw to it that Rosita Chavez was entertained while Mrs. Castelleno was upstairs with Hatfield."

"That's interesting." *I wonder if it went any further than that?* Corcoran drained his coffee and got to his feet. "Talk to Jimmy Henderson, Tony. I'll put in a good word for you too. Thank you for this conversation, it's been a big help." They shook hands and Corcoran made his way slowly back to the office, letting his mind roam over all this new information.

He remembered that he never met Mrs. Phelps and had a hard time even remembering what she might look like. Was she tall, short, thin, heavy? He simply couldn't remember. *No wonder Phelps was intrigued by Maria Castelleno and at the same time, Phelps's name hasn't come up from Castelleno or Rosita Chavez. And our fine district attorney would have the ability to hire his dirty work done. He's not the kind to bash someone's head in with a rock, though.*

Corcoran found Lou Foster in the office but the sheriff out. "Have a chat with Mose Willoughby?"

"He's sure that Oakley killed Hatfield. Doc Whidby's

back there with him now. Infection in the ear wound. It seems Willoughby and Oakley had decided to bump off Sawyer and Hatfield and do the bank robbery themselves. When Oakley didn't ride out with the group Willoughby knew the outlaw stayed behind to kill Hatfield."

"Well, at least some things make sense around here. Interesting that he talks to you. All I get is some nasty cursing."

"He doesn't like anyone touching the area where his ear used to be."

Corcoran had to laugh right out. "You're gonna do just fine with that badge, young 'un. Have any idea where the sheriff might be?"

"He went to talk with Ed Graves, the attorney. The doctor told the sheriff that Graves remembered something important and wanted to see you. Since you weren't here, the sheriff went."

"Good. I think I'll mosey up that way myself. Hold down the fort, Deputy Foster," Corcoran chuckled turning around for the door. The springtime warmth felt good on his walk up the hill to Ed Graves' office, which did double duty as his home, a Victorian masterpiece. The Graves House, as it was called, stood two stories high with enough classic architecture, newel posts, fancy woodwork, and scrollwork to keep an artisan busy for a month.

Graves answered the door almost immediately. "Saw you coming, Corcoran. Come in. We could use another set of opinions in here." Graves led him into a small sitting room off the main room and Corcoran was surprised to find the banker, Anderson, at the table with Ed Connor.

"Mr. Anderson, sheriff, hope I'm not interrupting."

"You're not, Corcoran," Connor said. "I'm glad you're here. Mr. Anderson was just telling us about his dealings with Gordon Hatfield. Sit down. You'll enjoy this." Connor motioned for Corcoran to sit and for Anderson to continue.

"When Hatfield arrived here a couple of years ago, he deposited a tidy sum of money with the bank," Anderson said. "I'm really not sure I should be divulging this information, but since the man is dead and involved in the fire that destroyed the Eureka House, I will. It's complicated so it would be best if you let me tell it out before asking questions."

Corcoran, Connor, and Graves all nodded. Graves stepped into his kitchen and came out with a bottle of bourbon. He poured generous amounts for each and sat back down.

"The Eureka House was in debt and Hatfield was able to pick it up for a reasonable price. What few people knew, though, the previous owner, Gattlin, Fred Gattlin, had a silent partner and that partner wished to keep his share of the business. Hatfield was more than pleased with the idea. After all, having the district attorney as your business partner certainly gives you a step up in the community."

Corcoran almost choked on his bourbon at the comment. "Phelps was Hatfield's partner? Good lord almighty. I just found out that Phelps was also one of the men seeing Maria Castelleno regularly. Damn!" The large man stood up and walked around the finely furnished great room, sipping his drink, almost talking to himself.

"When are those insurance men arriving?" Corcoran asked. "Are they aware of what Mr. Anderson just said?" Corcoran looked at Anderson. "Is Phelps on the fire insurance papers? We have to put a tail on the man, sheriff." Corcoran's mind was on fire putting all of this into place.

Phelps has a relationship with the dead woman. Phelps is a partner with the dead man who had a relationship with the dead woman. Phelps is connected by legal partnership with the man accused of burning their business to the ground. And on top of all that, Rosita may have a relationship with the arsonist in question.

"The insurance papers are made out in the name of the partnership, Corcoran," Anderson said. "At this moment, until a court establishes otherwise, the owner of the business is the beneficiary."

Corcoran looked at Anderson. *The owner of the business? Wouldn't that be Phelps? Why didn't he just say that?* The big deputy shook his head, slightly, but didn't pursue the matter.

"The San Francisco men are scheduled on tomorrow morning's train," Connor said.

Corcoran stood up, drained his glass, wanted five more like it, nodded to the group, and walked out the door. *Where the hell do I start?*

CHAPTER FIFTEEN

"JIMMY," Corcoran said, walking into the Bonanza Club. "Your favorite deputy sheriff needs help. Desperately needs help." A couple of hard-rock miners at the bar chuckled but knew better than to say anything.

"Whiskey, not beer, coming up," Jimmy Henderson laughed. "What now, Corcoran?"

"I'll get the easy one out first and then we'll plod through the other. Tony Soma needs a job. Now," Corcoran said, "time to get serious." Corcoran took his glass of whiskey to the far end of the bar, away from others' ears. In a small town rumors run rampant and once one gets started, there's no stopping it.

"Let's talk Bill Phelps, our Eureka County district attorney. All I really know about the man is he all but worships those who have direct ties to Virginia City and San Francisco. Idolizes them, which would embarrass me to death."

"His wife as well," Henderson said. "Phelps is a strange man, Terrence. He says his wife is cold, unwilling to fulfill her wifely duties, while at the same time the women who work for me do what they can to shy away from him. He's rough with women. After a woman has said 'no' to him five times or more, he's still coming on to them."

"I've just learned that myself," Corcoran said. He didn't say anything about Phelps being in partnership with Gordon Hatfield but instead asked Henderson about Phelps's financial condition.

"As district attorney he draws a county salary, but I remember when he arrived in the county, he was almost destitute. He took any and every case that came his way to make a dollar. Represented Alphonso Castelleno's mining company in a couple of juicy lawsuits. That's where he made his reputation and his money."

Corcoran thought that that's where he became infatuated with Maria as well. "Was he married at this time?"

"No, Terrence. No woman was safe from his advances back then. He made a trip to Virginia City and came back with a wife." Jimmy Henderson scowled and gave Corcoran a long look. "What's brought all this on?"

"You haven't mentioned anything about Phelps investing in local businesses, or what other means of income he might have. I've heard a rumor or two." Corcoran learned a long time ago not to divulge information about cases unless he wanted everyone in town to know about it.

"He owned some stock in the Castelleno Mine as payment for his work on their behalf but other than that, I haven't heard of anything." Henderson poured the two of them some more whiskey before continuing.

"He did some work for the previous owner of the Eureka House but I'm not sure how he was paid for that. After the election, he drank there more often than here. I think those two girls Hatfield had working for him were more to his liking."

Corcoran chuckled but didn't say anything about the partnerships. "Well, you've answered a couple of questions, Jimmy. Is Rosita in the kitchen?"

"Cindy is. Not sure about Rosita."

"I'll come back later, then," Corcoran said. He drained the glass and ambled out the door. *Two little talks with two of my favorite bartenders and I've got a huge and ugly picture of our district attorney right now. Castelleno's hatred of Hatfield didn't extend to Phelps. Is it possible Phelps's encounters with Maria were unknown to the man? Or was there something else going on?*

———

CORCORAN WALKED BACK to the sheriff's office to talk with George Atkins, the faro dealer. Lou Foster was writing up some reports when he arrived. "Everything fine with our prisoners?"

"The infection in Willoughby's wound isn't getting better and George Atkins had a visitor, Terrence. Rosita Chavez was here a little while ago. I did as you and the sheriff said to do. Wouldn't let her in the cell and made her stand back from the bars. I stayed in the area to observe but not close enough to hear what was said."

"Sometimes I don't like my own rules," Corcoran laughed. "Wish you could have heard. What was Atkins's reaction? Was she friendly coming in? Tell me everything, Lou."

"You don't seem pleased by this," Foster said.

"Surprised is all. Four conversations in a row have surprised me and I'm getting tired of it. I've learned things in the last several hours that I would never have considered and all of what I've learned is having an effect on my investigation of Maria Castelleno's death." He plopped down behind the sheriff's desk, opened the bottom left-hand drawer and pulled out Sheriff Connor's flask.

"Start talking, Deputy Foster."

Foster didn't really have a lot to say other than Rosita Chavez was amiable when she arrived but left in a huff. That George Atkins seemed glad to see her when she walked into the cell area but cussed loud and long when she left.

"Interesting," Corcoran said. "Maybe it's my turn to get Atkins all riled up, eh? You weren't able to hear any of the conversation?"

"They seemed to be whispering right up until she left and he started cussing," Foster said.

Corcoran slipped the flask back in the drawer and walked into the cell area. "Everyone comfortable back here? Get you anything? Maybe a floozy or two? Some good whiskey? The cell door key?"

"Go to hell, Corcoran," Willoughby snarled. Atkins just harrumphed some.

"Bad attitude, boys. George, come up to the bars. Got a question or two for you."

Atkins sat down on his bunk instead and Corcoran

smiled at him. He turned back, waved at Foster to come in, pulled the rack of keys off the wall, and opened the cell door. "Lock me in, Lou. Mr. Atkins and I need to talk some. Don't leave, I might want back out soon." He handed the keys and his revolver to Foster.

"Don't know why you wanted this to be done the hard way. But, if that's what you want, it's fine with me." Corcoran stood, legs slightly spread, in front of the sitting Atkins. "Tell me about you and Rosita Chavez, Mr. Atkins. She is a lovely girl, knows her way around a kitchen. A man could do a lot worse."

Corcoran paused and gave George Atkins a long look. "Something bothering you, Atkins? You're looking at some hard time at the Carson City Prison, old man. You killed a man and burned down a business. Ain't nothing you can do or say to make that change. Talking some might make you feel better, though."

Atkins gave Willoughby a look, then turned his eyes to Corcoran and the deputy got the message loud and clear. Corcoran nodded to Foster who unlocked the cell and escorted the two into the front office.

"Sit down, George. Coffee?" Atkins nodded and took a seat near the stove. "What's on your mind?"

"Me and Rosita were going to run away after the fire but now she tells me she won't wait for me to get out of prison. She said she's going to make up with that damn fool Castelleno and be his wife."

"That's what all the howling was about?" Foster said. "You should feel lucky, not angry."

Corcoran chuckled. "I can't help you with your legal or your love problems, George, but you might be able to help me. What kind of part did Bill Phelps play at the Eureka House?"

"Phelps? The district attorney? He drank there. Never gambled. I don't understand."

"Neither do I," Corcoran said. "You wanted to say something back there. I doubt it was about Rosita."

"Hatfield had a partner, and he didn't want the partner to know that he was responsible for the building burning down. Didn't want Knight or me to ever mention that he was behind the fire."

"Did he say who that partner was?" *I just asked him about Phelps and he didn't say a word. Did Hatfield have other partners?*

"He never said who the partner was. Said it would all come out but we were being paid to set the blaze and to keep our mouths shut."

Corcoran had Foster take Atkins back to his cell and sat down with another cup of coffee. *One more knot in the wood, eh? Rosita wants to marry Castelleno, the man who beat her when she didn't stop his wife from dallying with other men? And the faro dealer who burned down the Eureka House doesn't seem to even know that Phelps was a partner in the operation? And Maria's murderer is walking amongst us.*

CHAPTER SIXTEEN

"YOU'RE NOT REALLY with me, Terrence." Cindy Cook was snuggled as close to the big man as she could get, but her nibbles on his ear, her passionate kisses, nor her roaming hands seemed to have much effect on the man. "Who are you thinking about, and it better not be Rosita."

Corcoran chuckled and wrapped his arms around the little vixen. "In a way, pretty lady, it is Rosita. It's also Bill Phelps, and a couple of men coming in from San Francisco in the morning." He unwrapped himself and sat up, throwing his legs off to the side of the bed. "Has Rosita said anything to you about Castelleno?"

"Other than the fact she wants to kill him?" She was scowling at Corcoran who was slipping into his clothes. "Don't go, Terrence. You need my loving."

"I do, but I can't get my mind off these problems. Tell me more about how she wants to kill Castelleno," he said.

"Oh, all right," she whimpered. She pulled the covers

up around her neck and smiled at him. "She really hates the man. He didn't do right by her at all, Terrence. Not right at all. She said she's going to marry him, poison him slowly, and get the mine and all his money. Could she do that?"

"She wouldn't be the first to take out a husband," he snickered. *So, what Atkins said is on the button.* "Don't you be getting ideas."

"Couldn't," she said. "We ain't married."

He gave her a long kiss and pat on her delightful bottom and walked out, chuckling. "Ain't married," he whispered. "And ain't gonna be." He walked toward his cabin down in the gulch watching the sky slowly come to life. *Rosita, Phelps, Afeldt, even Florencio, are my primary suspects right now. Even though he's dead, Hatfield is a suspect. Is Rosita's plan just a way to get even, to pay back for the beatings? Or, did she kill Maria with this plan in place? Was she spending time with Castelleno while Maria was off with others?*

But then we have to factor good old Bill Phelps in. Married and messing around with Castelleno's wife, even talking about it with his partner, Hatfield. Any of that gets out, goodbye to his political career. There has been talk about Phelps running for a seat in the state senate.

Corcoran hurried to his cabin to eat and get ready to meet the insurance investigators at the train station later. The cabin was rudimentary at best. Two rooms, one with a bed and Franklin stove, the other with a table and chairs and a wood-fired cookstove. In the bedroom, clothing hung on hooks and nails or was folded on shelves. There was one window in each room, one lamp in each room, and no indication that a woman had ever been inside the cabin.

His questions never let up, his mind never slowed down. *One wayward wife and how many lives are affected? I could really use some serious help on this little problem.*

———

"Rosita Chavez wants to marry and then slowly poison Castelleno?" Sheriff Ed Connor and Corcoran were on their horses riding down onto the valley floor to meet the train. "She has reason, but she can't be that stupid, can she? To actually tell someone?"

"Bill Phelps has had an ongoing affair with Maria, as well," Corcoran said. "He and Hatfield used to compare notes after their clandestine evenings with the woman. That's crude, but the whole thing is crude. Does this go further than just two or five men having their way with the mine owner's wife? Is there something else?"

"You've got more than a platter full right now, Corcoran. You don't need to look for more." Connor sat silent for a moment, enjoying the view across the Diamond Valley. "What else would there be anyway?"

"I don't know. Is the murder of Maria Castelleno connected in any way to the Phelps-Hatfield partnership? Was Phelps aware that Hatfield was planning to burn down the Eureka House? Was Phelps aware of Hatfield's plan to rob the Eureka Bank? And, how does Rosita Chavez play into the damn mess?"

"Yeah, as I said, you've got a platter full to work from." Connor never took his eyes off the vista spread out in front of the two. "We spend a lot of time working stolen beef crimes, Indian predation, and bloody drunks blowing their pay on the weekends, Corcoran—we're gonna actually earn our pay on this case."

Connor smiled, took a quick look north and saw the smoke from the Eureka and Palisades Railway train slowly moving across the plain. "What do you suppose these yahoos from San Francisco are actually going to do?"

"From what Ed Graves said, they're going to pay off on the fire. My question is, what are you going to do, sheriff?"

"Fight 'em, Corcoran. That's what we are going to do." He put a lot of emphasis on the we part of that comment. "Another question, my friend, is what is Phelps going to do? Do you think he was aware of what Hatfield was up to? Do you suppose it was Phelps who killed Hatfield in order to get that payoff?"

"Our district attorney has a lot of questions that need to be answered, sheriff. Atkins said the partner wasn't aware of the planned arson. Are you calling for a hearing on the matter? Would Justice of the Peace Trimble head such a hearing?"

"No, it would be a sheriff's hearing, Corcoran, which could lead to a full court hearing. Ed Graves was Hatfield's attorney and Bill Phelps was Hatfield's partner. No, this will be my opportunity to question all parties. I've already sent a request to the county commission to hire an outside attorney in case charges are filed. Phelps certainly can't be involved."

"I talked with George Atkins, and he didn't seem to

be aware that Phelps was a partner in the Eureka House business but did believe there was a partner. I wonder if there are others? Have you looked at how the business is listed with the county?" Corcoran was thinking that when this case was over there would be openings for various county offices, in particular district attorney.

"As near as I can figure it, only Hatfield and Phelps were involved, and Phelps's name is hard to find in the documents. If there are others, I can't find them," Connor said.

They dismounted in front of the train depot as the big steamer pulled up with a loud, whistle blowing, steam-venting stop. "Love the way they do that," Connor said. "Makes you want to be right up there in that engine pulling ropes and throwing levers."

"You're a romantic old codger, sheriff. Let's go find our insurance investigators." Corcoran laughed and held the door open for his boss.

———

THE TWO INVESTIGATORS couldn't be missed. Very few men in Eureka wore black pinstriped suits and bowler-style hats. The two men weren't wearing boots and would rue that mistake. Their patent leather shoes shone in the spring sunshine, at least until they met their first mud puddle.

"Good morning," Sheriff Connor said. "I'm Eureka County Sheriff Ed Connor and this is my chief deputy, Terrence Corcoran. Welcome to our little back-country village."

Corcoran couldn't hold in the chuckle, caught Connor's wrinkled eyes, and knew this just might be fun, dealing with the big-city attorneys. "Good morning," the taller of the two said. "I'm Richard Wellington and this is Arthur Bellows. We represent the Lighthouse Insurance Company of San Francisco. I believe we have rooms at something called the Bonanza Club. Bring our bags, please."

"I'm a courteous gentleman of the old school, sir," Sheriff Connor said, "and the elected sheriff of this county. I'm sure you can manage your own baggage. You probably have plenty." Connor winked at Corcoran and continued. "There will be a hearing in the conference room of the Eureka County Courthouse at one o'clock this afternoon."

Connor nodded, turned, and walked off the platform to the hitching rack. "Arrogant little bastard's gonna get a black eye by the time this is over." He never looked back as he mounted and rode off up the hill to town.

Corcoran smiled to the two insurance attorneys and followed the sheriff. It was Bellows who called him back. "How are we to get to town, sir?"

"Shorty Johnson, over there in the red sweater, runs a hack for every train that comes to town. He'll be more than happy to help you. See you at one." He turned again and again was called back.

"Are you the same Terrence Corcoran who was involved in what became known as the Lahontan Valley War?" Bellows was tanned, his hands weren't velvet soft as were those of Wellington, and his shoulders were broad and strong.

"I am, sir." Corcoran said.

"I ended up representing the Pyramid Lake Paiute," Bellows said. "Because of you they were treated well. I never had the good fortune of meeting you during the proceedings and ended up moving from Carson City to San Francisco because of the ordeal. It's a pleasure, sir," Bellows said, holding out his hand.

"It is, indeed," Corcoran said. They shook hands, Corcoran smiled at the man, nodded to Wellington, and walked off to find Dude for the ride back to town. *This is the first good turn of events in this entire situation. Bellows will be straight, that's for sure. Wellington will just be a big-city ass and Connor will eat him alive.* He waved to the two as he rode off.

———

"THIS FIRST MEETING is simply for all of us to have an opportunity to go over everything involved in the loss of the Eureka House," Sheriff Connor said. "Ed Graves is the late Gordon Hatfield's attorney, and you gentlemen, Mr. Wellington and Mr. Bellows, represent the insurance company that Hatfield engaged. We'll not call witnesses at this meeting but will in future meetings."

"We should be able to wrap this up in less than an hour, I would think," Wellington said. "We're prepared. Why call witnesses?"

"Mainly because there are multiple crimes involved in the fire that destroyed the Eureka House, including arson, sir." Connor was quiet in his response but his strength was evident.

"I simply don't believe this nonsense of arson. And surely Mr. Hatfield was not involved," Wellington said.

"That's exactly why we'll be having these meetings. More than likely this initial meeting will lead us into judicial hearings. As far as the arson question is concerned, I'm holding one of the men that Hatfield hired to set the fires, and there is ample evidence, including murder, to back up his testimony."

"Who besides this alleged arsonist will we be hearing from?" Arthur Bellows asked. "And why are you conducting these initial hearings? Shouldn't the district attorney be present?"

"May I, sheriff?" Ed Graves asked, and Connor nodded. "Unfortunately, the district attorney is also Gordon Hatfield's partner and would be recipient of the insurance payout. As Hatfield's attorney and with help from the sheriff, we have asked the county commission to appoint someone to represent the county when this becomes a judicial hearing."

"Considering what we've heard in this meeting," Arthur Bellows said, "I suggest we move directly to a judicial hearing. There's a lot at stake here and I wasn't aware that Mr. Hatfield's partner was the county attorney."

"Nor was I," Wellington said. "I'm still willing to make the payoff. I simply don't believe Gordon Hatfield was capable of arson."

"I plan to prove he was," Sheriff Connor said. "So. It seems it will be up to Justice of the Peace Tommy Trimble to set a hearing date and time. Thank you for being here." Connor got up, shuffled some papers around, and watched the two big-city attorneys walk out of the conference room.

"How did it go, Corcoran? Did I do things right?"

"As always, Ed," Corcoran said. "That Wellington will be an ass in court, but the one who will have all the strength will be Art Bellows. He finished off in court what I started with the Paiutes several years ago. He's a tiger, Ed, but honest. Wellington won't care much about truth or evidence, but Bellows will."

I want to go at this as if we were at a full trial, not a judicial hearing, Terrence," Connor said. "Evidence, evidence, and more evidence. A good time to Lou Foster to understand the value of evidence. I want those prisoners' interviews written up—I want this to be so strong that Mr. Wellington's eyes swim."

"I'll get right on it," Corcoran said not even trying to hold in his laughter. "Right away, boss."

CHAPTER SEVENTEEN

"THAT WAS A GUNSHOT," Connor yelled as he and Corcoran walked out of the conference room. People were pouring from the courthouse and surrounding homes and businesses. Corcoran, leading the charge, spotted Ed Graves sprawled in the mud and blood at the side of the road, Arthur Bellows at his side.

"He's dead, Corcoran," Bellows said.

"Never saw the shooter," Richard Wellington said. Wellington's face was ghostly white, his hands were shaking, and his eyes were whipping about as if searching for the shooter. "The shot came from somewhere behind that white house over there." Wellington was as frightened a man as Corcoran had ever seen, almost crying as he spoke.

"I was standing right there talking with the man. That could be me in the mud there," Wellington said.

"Why would Hatfield's attorney be shot?" Bellows asked.

"If the shot was aimed at Graves, it was probably

because he knows too much about Hatfield, his partner or partners, and how the arson was planned," Corcoran said. "On the other hand, if it was for you, Mr. Wellington, we'd have to do some pondering on that, eh? Send for the doc," Corcoran said to Ed Connor and sprinted across the street, leaped the fence, and raced around behind the house and into an empty yard.

The yard was muddy, and Corcoran found boot prints at the edge of the building. "That's a good thirty-five yard shot so I'd guess it was from a rifle," Corcoran muttered. Bellows, who had followed the lawman nodded.

"You really caught Wellington off guard when you suggested the shot may have been aimed at him." Bellows was doing his best not to chuckle some, and Corcoran just smiled. The wise man knew he didn't need to say anything more.

The two men spent several minutes looking for prints leading away from the yard and came up empty. "Anybody see anything?" Corcoran asked when they returned to where the body was. "Anything at all?" He didn't get an answer. "Take care of things here, sheriff. I'm going to try and find Mr. Phelps."

"Want company?" Bellows asked.

"Damn right. I like your style, Bellows."

It was a quick two-block walk to where Bill Phelps had his home and Corcoran used that time to bring Bellows up to date on the myriad cases he was working on. "Somehow, all of that is connected," he chuckled.

"That's a real mess," Bellows laughed. He stopped short and pointed at the walkway that led to Phelps's front door. "That's mud, Corcoran."

Corcoran, almost at a run, followed the muddy prints that led around to the side of the building. "Damn," he said, pulling up short, looking at a pair of muddy boots sitting next to an apple tree. Corcoran held up his hands to keep Bellows from coming too far and bent down trying to see if he could find some footprints.

"Looks almost like this was planned," Bellows said. "That crushed grass and those toppled rocks seem to want us to follow off across the yard and back out toward the street."

"You spent some time as an investigator before becoming an attorney? You sure have this scene figured out. Someone wants us to believe Bill Phelps was the shooter. Something's wrong, though. Do you see it?"

"Tell me, Corcoran."

"The footprints are smaller than the foot that would fit in that boot. The shooter wore oversize boots on purpose."

"You're thinking a woman did this?" Bellows asked and bent down to look again at the crushed grass and then the boots. "You're good, Corcoran."

"A woman or a small man. I would imagine there was a pair of shoes hidden right over there and our shooter could be anywhere by now. Let's see if our district attorney is home. We're not smashing an ethics barrier, are we?"

"No, you're being a gentleman bringing me to meet Mr. Hatfield's partner," Bellows said. There was a definite grin and gleam in his eye and Corcoran had to chuckle walking up to Phelps's front door. He rapped hard and heard footsteps approaching.

"Yes? Who is it?" A woman's muffled voice asked from inside the closed door. There was no attempt to open the door. Corcoran cocked his head slightly and looked at Bellows.

I've heard that voice. Corcoran's eyes were narrowed in deep thought. *It's not Mrs. Phelps, she's out of town and they don't have help. Are we busting up a tryst?*

"Eureka County Deputy Sheriff Corcoran to see District Attorney Bill Phelps," Corcoran called out.

"Mr. Phelps isn't receiving guests today," the voice said. "He only see visitors at his office on Tuesdays."

Corcoran looked at Bellows and shrugged his shoulders as a question. Bellows cocked his head as an answer. *I've heard that voice before.* The thought wouldn't go away. *She's trying to change the way she sounds. Who is that?* Corcoran said to the woman inside, "Very well. Tell the gentleman his insurance attorney is in town looking for him."

The door was flung open, and Bill Phelps stepped onto the porch. "Insurance attorney? I don't understand."

"How do you do," Art Bellows said. "I'm Arthur Bellows with Lighthouse Insurance Company of San Francisco here to determine if we should pay off the fire claim on the Eureka House. You were Gordon Hatfield's partner, right?"

Phelps took in a quick breath, looking back and forth between Bellows and Corcoran, and hesitated for some moments before clearing his throat. "Um, uh, well, yes. Mr. Hatfield and I were partners in the operation. We didn't let that become general knowledge, however."

"General knowledge or not, as his partner you may be the beneficiary of the claim if it is upheld," Bellows said.

Corcoran glanced down and saw that Phelps was wearing bedroom slippers, not shoes or boots, and that his feet were of a size to fit his large body, dashing that theory. "May we come in, please? There's been a shooting involving Hatfield's attorney and I have a few questions for you."

"I'd really rather not," Phelps said, but Art Bellows simply stepped around the gentleman and was inside that fast. "Please," Phelps finally said, stepping aside for Corcoran. "Come in."

How easily a man of his size, of his standing in the community, could be beaten down always amazed Terrence Corcoran. Here is William Phelps, attorney-at-law, district attorney for the county of Eureka, Nevada, and so easily pushed aside by Art Bellows, who isn't even a lawman, doesn't wear a badge, but may have money to offer in the form of an insurance claim.

Corcoran stopped instantly when inside. "Rosita Chavez," he said. "Good afternoon." *She did a good job disguising her voice. Well, well.*

"Miss Chavez takes care of the house while Mrs. Phelps is out of town, now that she no longer works for Mr. Castelleno," Phelps was quick to say.

And all of that inside just a few days since she was fired, Corcoran smiled at the thought. *She's cooking at the Bonanza Club and cleaning for Bill Phelps? I don't think so. But what is she doing for Bill Phelps? Is she killing people? Or just offering some womanly comfort while his wife is out of town?*

Corcoran noticed that Rosita's blouse wasn't

buttoned properly and that, she too, was not wearing shoes or boots. Her tiny feet were encased in bedroom slippers as well. *Hiding her shoes or boots, he's not wearing any, but I don't see any splashed mud either. This is most interesting.*

"What is this all about," Phelps said. "A shooting?"

"Mr. Hatfield's attorney was shot, Mr. Phelps," Art Bellows said. "He was standing next to my partner at the time. We'll get into that a little later, I suppose." Bellows looked at Corcoran. "Why don't you explain the hearing process, Deputy Corcoran?"

"Yes, of course," Corcoran said. He caught the quick smile from Bellows. "Sheriff Connor was going to hold a series of hearings for the benefit of the insurance investigators, but that program has certainly changed with Graves's murder. I'm sure the hearings will be held by the justice of the peace. Or an appointed district judge."

"What kind of hearings would that be? The Eureka House surely burned to the ground," Phelps said.

"It surely did," Corcoran said. "The question that will be asked and answered is whether or not the fire was caused by arson, who might have been responsible for the conflagration, and whether or not the insurance company will pay off on the claim. It would be to your benefit to remain in Eureka until after the hearings."

"Arson? who would benefit from arson?" Phelps said and quickly realized that wasn't the thing to say.

"You, for one," Bellows said. "Well, we'd best get back and save poor Mr. Wellington."

THE WALK back to the courthouse found the two rather animated in their conversation. "No boots or shoes to be seen," Bellows said. "Both in slippers and she not correctly buttoned. Were those buttons misplaced for our benefit? Did that woman just run in the house, ditch her boots and the rifle, put slippers on, then unbutton and rebutton improperly?"

"Best guess I've heard," Corcoran said. "There's a lot wrong with her being there and it doesn't have anything to do with Phelps's marriage. She has told several people within the last day or two that she was planning to make a play for Castelleno and then poison the old man for his mine and wealth."

"Oh, yeah," Bellows said. "And now, she's killing the attorney of one of the men who played games with Mrs. Castelleno and maybe at the suggestion of another of the men involved with the shady lady. Where oh where are we being led, Corcoran?"

"I like the 'we' stuff, Bellows. Rosita Chavez has questions pinned on every inch of her body, sir." The two were walking slow, letting everything they just learned sink in. *Bellows might be onto something here.* Corcoran's mind could almost be heard grinding away. *Are Rosita and Phelps in a conspiracy to take over Castelleno's mine? But why kill Ed Graves? Because he knew too much, that's why. Knew too much about the partnership of Phelps and Hatfield? Or too much about something else?* Corcoran almost had to shake his head to slow down his thought process.

"She appeared to be very good friends with Maria Castelleno but tells everyone she hated the woman." Corcoran said. "It appears that Castelleno beat her badly, although he denies it, and she tells everyone she's going to marry the old beast. And, she despised Gordon Hatfield and Bill Phelps, she said, for their shenanigans with Maria but seemed to be mighty close to Phelps just now."

"Just how much money is involved here, Corcoran?" Bellows asked. "I've never yet run into something like this that didn't have a large pot of gold at its center. Some of what you've talked about appears to have been well planned and other parts seem to have come off the wall, so to speak."

"I agree," Corcoran said. "Money? The Castelleno Mine property is worth hundreds of thousands of dollars, if not millions. Castelleno is worth an incredible amount of money. He's invested in ranch property up and down the Diamond Valley, owns part of the railroad, has timber interests. If she did as she has indicated, she would be worth millions, Bellows." Corcoran surprised himself when he spoke of the wealth involved.

"We're almost back at the courthouse. How much of what we've learned should we divulge?"

"You mean to Richard Wellington?" Corcoran nodded and Bellows smiled. "Not much. He's positive there was no arson, as you've heard."

"Think he might be tied up with Phelps or with Hatfield? Whew." Corcoran wiped sweat from his forehead and shook the deep, red curls back in place. "Certainly a fine reason to have Ed Graves murdered. I don't think there's an end to this little murder case of mine. It all started on such a lovely day for a picnic."

CHAPTER EIGHTEEN

"ABOUT TIME YOU TWO GOT BACK," Sheriff Ed Connor said. "Find out anything from Phelps?"

Connor was standing next to Doctor Whidby after Whidby loaded Graves's body into a wagon. "Where's Wellington?" Corcoran asked.

"Went back to the hotel in a huff," Connors said. "Well?"

"Let's go have a cold beer, sheriff, and I'll bring you up to date."

"I'll go find my partner," Bellows said. "Let's have supper together, Corcoran. I've got a couple of ideas."

"You'd best be with us, sheriff. We got us a deep pit filled with stuff we don't know anything about," Corcoran laughed.

The cold beer turned into several as Corcoran took his time trying to explain what he and Bellows found at the Phelps' house. "As I said," Corcoran said, "we've got a mess. Rosita is at the heart of everything, and right now Phelps might be the key that would unlock this conspiracy. I'm not sure we can accept anything the woman might say as coming close to the truth. What she says and what she does are never the same things."

Connor sat quiet the entire time, trying to absorb all that Corcoran was laying out for him. "With the amount of wealth involved, with more lives at stake, and almost no credible evidence in hand, what are you planning to do?" Connor shook his head and took a long look out the front window of the Bonanza Club. "I doubt Castelleno would agree with any of this. There isn't enough evidence to question either Rosita or Phelps, and anything Ed Graves might have wanted to tell us won't be told now."

"Always thinking positive, eh sheriff?" Corcoran snickered and took a long drink of his beer. "Graves's murder is an open case, Ed. Do we need a court order to search his offices and home? He did tell us about the Hatfield-Phelps partnership. I rather doubt we'd get any kind of court order to search Phelps's home."

Sheriff Ed Connor laughed and shook his head. "No, not Phelps's, but you have every right to search Ed Graves's place. You and Lou Foster need to do that as soon as you can. Where does this Bellows fellow fit in? Insurance investigator? Or something more?"

"My guess is something more, sheriff," Corcoran said. "But I don't know what direction that something more would be. He is one hell of an investigator, though, and I'm sure he's on our side. He and Wellington, although working together, aren't close at all. Wellington will throw stones in our investigation, I'm sure. He's not thinking a half inch past the burning of the Eureka House."

"Is there a reason for that?" Connor asked. "If Phelps and Rosita are conspiring, would they include a third? An insurance investigator? Between the insurance payoff for the Eureka House and acquiring the Castelleno property by way of poison, there's one hell of a chunk of change involved."

"You, Bellows, and I are all thinking along the same lines, Ed. Wellington, if involved, would only be in seeing to it that the insurance on the Eureka House would be paid. He isn't intelligent enough to be involved in the Castelleno conspiracy. He needs to be watched closely, in any case," Corcoran said.

———

BELLOWS MADE his way upstairs at the Bonanza Club and knocked on Richard Wellington's hotel room door. He heard movement in the room, but no one answered the door and he knocked again, louder. Still no answer and Bellows grabbed the knob and twisted it, finding it unlocked. Wellington was sitting on the bed, fully clothed, and William Phelps was standing near the window.

"How dare you barge in, uninvited," Wellington said. "My God, man, have you no manners?"

"Manners include responding to a knock on the door, Dick." Bellows turned to the Eureka County district attorney. "Hello, Mr. Phelps. Here to discuss the question of arson? Or the murder of your partner's attorney?" He looked at Wellington. "That is the purpose of this meeting, isn't it?"

"I do not appreciate your barging in here, Mr. Bellows, and the purpose of Mr. Phelps's visit isn't of your concern." He coughed, nodded to Phelps, and scowled at Bellows. "Now if you'll excuse us."

"I will, Dick, but San Francisco will need to know about this meeting. Highly unusual, sir. It must be included in my report." Bellows turned and walked off, leaving the hotel room door wide open. *This is exactly what Corcoran and I were alluding to. I'd best find him soonest and then get a wire off to the office. Now I understand why Wellington simply wouldn't discuss the facts of the arson.*

The telegraph office was across the street from the sheriff's office and Bellows stopped there first, sent two quick wires to San Francisco, and walked across the main street to find Corcoran. Ed Connor was behind his old oak desk writing. A flask and tin cup sat close at hand.

"Bellows," Connor said. "Corcoran and I spent some time talking about you. Come in. Grab a cup over there."

"I'd like the two of you to be together when I say why I've come to the office. Is he about?"

"He's in the back with Deputy Lou Foster. They'll be right out. Want a shot of good bourbon in that coffee?"

Bellows nodded, took the hefty shot of whiskey, and sat down near the stove. "Been a hell of a day, sheriff. This might simply knock me out and hold me down." He took a sip of good bourbon and smiled. "What do you know about Bill Phelps? The insurance company doesn't know much about the man other than the obvious. He's an attorney and the county DA, but not much more."

"There isn't much more to know, I'm afraid. He came to

us by way of Virginia City and that's about all we know about the man. During the election there wasn't a lot he discussed about his background. Apparently, it doesn't include criminal activity or I'm sure it would have been brought up."

"Ah, Corcoran," Bellows said as Corcoran and Foster came into the office. "Just talking about Bill Phelps. I went to see Dick Wellington at the hotel and found Phelps in his room as well. It's time for me to tell you a little more about why I'm along on this visit."

"I thought there might be more to you than insurance investigator," Corcoran said. He had a smile on his face and nodded at Connor as if to say, 'I told you'. "This is Deputy Sheriff Lou Foster, Art. Gonna be one hell of a lawman very soon."

"Lighthouse Insurance Company has me on their records as an investigator, but they hired me to investigate Richard Wellington rather than our customers. Wellington has settled several recent and large arson cases in favor of our clients despite evidence to the contrary and I've been hired to end it." He took a long breath, filled his coffee cup, and added some flavoring from Connor's flask.

"I'm a private investigator, and this situation you have going on here will end Dick Wellington's career in the insurance business." There was a gentle but confident chuckle with the comment.

"Our investigation," Corcoran said, "is sure a hell of a lot broader than insurance fraud. A lot of dead people are involved, more than one conspiracy is involved, and what your man knows about it all might be the key to its unraveling. He doesn't seem to be a dangerous kind of criminal. Does he have violence in his background?"

"No," Bellows said. "Not that I've come across. Other than being a part of the conspiracy that burns buildings down, he isn't violent. He splits insurance claims with people who burn their property to the ground. This particular case is much more violent than anything he's been involved in. So many people dead and some not even related to the fire."

"This is most interesting," Connor said. "Bill Phelps, the district attorney, not known for being the least bit violent and Dick Wellington, the insurance investigator, also not a violent man, both involved up to their necks in multiple deaths surrounding a known arson." Connor looked around the room.

"You need to remember every single word that's being uttered," Corcoran said to Lou Foster. "This is how it all gets put together." Foster nodded and shook his head as well.

"There may just be another person that we don't know," Connor continued. "Someone who stands to gain considerably from the ashes of the Eureka House and the deaths of Hatfield and Graves."

"Whoever killed Graves ran to Bill Phelps's house," Corcoran said. "Knowing they would be safe? Or giving someone the idea that Phelps was involved? My first thought was, actually still is, Rosita Chavez."

"She's so small, Terrence," Connor said. "You said the shooter was wearing oversize boots and would have been carrying a heavy rifle as well. To and from the murder. Is she capable of that?"

"Come up with a better suspect, let me know about it," Corcoran smiled. "I'm sure it wasn't Phelps. He's just too big a man to leave boot prints the size we saw. You might be right, sheriff. There might very well be someone we don't know involved in this. Another Hatfield partner?"

Corcoran looked at Connor, then Foster before continuing. "Deputy Foster and I were about to visit Ed Graves's house and see what we can find. Care to join us? I know it's late, that this has been a long damn day, but I don't want that house to sit empty for the night."

"No, you don't. Sure as hell what you're looking for would be gone by morning, stolen, or burned. If we're lucky, Mr. Graves was a stickler for filing, and we'll know a lot more about this partnership between Gordon Hatfield and Bill Phelps. I wonder what Phelps or Hatfield offered Wellington—what the percentage was— to deny the arson and have the claim paid off?"

"I doubt we'll find that," Foster said right out. He reddened some at the chuckles that followed but also saw the nod from Sheriff Connor. Connor liked what he was seeing and hearing from the young man.

Corcoran, Foster, and Bellows headed up the street for Ed Graves's house and Sheriff Connor walked toward the Bonanza Club. "Think I might just run into either Phelps or Wellington? Hope you boys have as much fun as I do."

CHAPTER NINETEEN

"WHERE DO WE START?" Lou Foster asked. The Graves home was also the attorney's office. He set aside one room, probably started out as a sitting room or sewing room, as his working office. It was crowded with a large desk and massive armchair, two chairs at the desk, and three filing cabinets. There were scattered sheets of paper spread across the desk, but it wasn't messy, just not quite fully organized.

"Best bet is you, Mr. Foster, sit in one of the chairs and go through all the papers on top of the desk," Bellows said. "Look for any reference to these names, Gordon Hatfield, William Phelps, and Eureka House. Mr. Corcoran and I will tackle these filing cabinets looking for the same."

Foster had a pained look on his face as he moved to gather all the papers on Graves's desk. "The exciting and dangerous life of an investigator, Mr. Foster," Corcoran chuckled. "Get used to it."

The sun had been down for some time, lamps were

lit, and stomachs were growling before Foster said, "Ah, now this is more like it. We may have found the original partnership papers, Corcoran." He had a full folder and laid it down on top of the now cleaned-off desk. "Those top two pages seem to be the agreement."

Corcoran took Graves's chair and read through the documents, smiling.

"It was sitting off to the side of the individual sheets of paper," Foster said.

"Graves had it out and was probably going to bring it to the court hearing," Bellows said. "Is there something extraordinary in the agreement, Corcoran?"

Terrence Corcoran started to say something when gunfire erupted from outside and a rock followed by a tied-off bundle of kerosene-soaked rags came through the office window. Bellows went down howling in pain as did Foster, and Corcoran found himself flat on the floor, bullets ripping though the walls and whining just over his head. He rolled across the floor to the torch and tried to fling it back through the broken window but was only able to catch the curtains on fire.

Continuing gunfire kept the big deputy flat on the floor and he watched, helplessly as one stray shot blew up one of the kerosene lamps near the desk. He rolled across the floor and managed to get hold of the partnership file and handed it to Foster. "Don't let go of this for anything."

That's more than one shooter. Too many shots coming too fast for just one person, and the rock and torch being thrown as well. This was well planned. Corcoran moved to where his other wounded companion was.

"Hang onto the file, Foster," Corcoran said and grabbed the big man by his ankles. "Grab Bellows by the feet and I'll get us out of here. It's gonna hurt." The fire was raging in just minutes and Corcoran was only making inches at a time, trying to drag the two wounded men across area rugs, knocking furniture out of the way.

"I can crawl," Bellows yelled out. "Save the youngster and the files." He rolled onto his stomach and snaked his way out of the room, leaving a trail of bloodstains. Foster wasn't able to help but had a death grip on the papers and file. The three men were flat on the floor in the living room of Graves's house, random shots were still being fired into the building and the first raucous clanging of fire bells could be heard above the roar of the fire.

"Gotta get us out of here," Corcoran mumbled. "You can crawl, Art. Head for the back door. Lou, can you move at all?" There was no answer and Corcoran froze, not wanting to think why. "Take these with you, Art, and get moving." He ripped the files from Foster's hands and shoved them at Bellows.

Got to get me and that kid out of here. Come on, Lou, don't you dare die on me. I got plans for you, buster. Corcoran stayed as low as he could get but realized there weren't any more gunshots, just the clanging of fire bells, and jumped to his feet. He grabbed Foster under the arms and dragged him through the kitchen and out the open back door, into a muddy yard behind the house. Bellows was stretched out under an apple tree, covered in mud.

"Fire boys ain't gonna get that out, Corcoran. Those shooters knew where we were in there too. This isn't the way Wellington works. There's a lot more to this than either one of us is thinking. A lot more."

Corcoran laughed right out. "I think we just met the sheriff's third man. How bad are you shot, Art? Lou, can you hear me? How bad is your wound? We got to get out of this yard and away from that building. I can hear the hose wagons coming now, but they'll attack the fire from the front, not knowin' we're back here."

"Go get help, Corcoran," Bellows said. "We're safe here for the time being."

"Check on that boy, Art. He's not made a sound. Not willing to lose him." Corcoran was on his feet and ran around to the front of the house. He sent one of the town's youngsters to fetch Doc Whidby and snared a couple more to help him get Art Bellows and Lou Foster out of danger. It wasn't but a few minutes and Sheriff Connor showed up.

"At least two people involved, sheriff," Corcoran said. "I'm sure they came to torch the building, found lamps on, and started shooting before throwing the torch in. The idea of a third partner is looking better every minute."

Corcoran and the sheriff sat down on the wet ground next to Bellows and Foster. "How you doing, Lou? Can you hear me?" Corcoran asked. Foster was bleeding from two bullet wounds, one high on his right shoulder and the other, just as high, in his chest.

Foster's slurred speech was all Corcoran needed. "He's alive, sheriff. Hope Doc Whidby gets here quickly. Ain't gonna lose this boy. He's just what this old department needs. He's gonna be a good lawman, Ed. A good one."

Connor saw the slightest grin on Foster's contorted face and smiled as well. "Yes he is, Terrence. Were you able to see anything?"

"Not a thing. Too busy trying to be a part of the carpet and the fire boys have destroyed anything we might have been able to see outside the building. Bellows took a nasty hit in his leg, but he's got the bleeding under control." Corcoran looked around at the continuing devastation. "I doubt they will save Graves's beautiful home. Two big buildings gone inside of a week. Ain't good, sheriff."

Corcoran saw Doc Whidby and waved him over. "Two more for you, Doc. At least these two are alive and kicking."

Whidby brought his wagon and with some help from a couple of the firefighters, got Bellows and Foster loaded up. Corcoran, Connor, and two firefighters followed Doctor Whidby to his combination home/office/hospital and got the patients inside. Corcoran grabbed the file that Bellows held and motioned for Connor.

"Let's go somewhere where we can read these papers, get some food in us, and have a barrel of whiskey on the side. Foster said these might be the original partnership papers. Is it possible that third name just might be in there? Graves had the file out on his desk. Everything else is ashes now."

THEY HAD to almost fight their way through the throng of meddlers to get to the Bonanza Club and found the place almost empty. "You start that fire, Corcoran? Killin' my business. Everyone wants to see the fire." Jimmy Henderson was half serious, half laughing as the two made their way to a table in the back, near the kitchen.

"Ed Graves's place, Jimmy," Sheriff Connor said. "Tell Cindy to just start bringing food and we'll tell her when to quit. Bring us a fresh bottle and join us. Have a question or two for you."

"You could have knocked some of the mud off before coming in," he said, walking off to get the bottle. "You're the third one tonight bringing me mud."

"Third?" Corcoran asked. "Who were the other two?"

"Rosita Chavez and one of the miners from Castelleno's. Not runnin' a bathhouse here," Henderson said.

"Never can really be sure when he's joking," Corcoran said. "We need to ask Cindy where Rosita went when she brings our food too. There were at least two people shooting into that building, into the room where we were."

Henderson brought a bottle and three glasses, pulled up a chair, and got right to the point. "Been right here all evening, sheriff."

"That's fine, Jimmy. Just fine. What I need to know, though, is everything you might know about Gordon Hatfield's business. How many partners did he have, how many people did he owe money to, and any other possible enemies or close friends he had."

"Man's dead, sheriff. Doubt if he started the fire." The little joke drew frowns from Corcoran and Connor and

Henderson got himself serious in a hurry. "Gordon Hatfield and I were never friends. He was in my place no more than twice that I know of and I visited his just the once when he opened it. He made it clear that I wasn't welcome." Jimmy Henderson took a minute to pour all the way around and sipped his.

"What I'm saying is, I don't know nothing about the man. It's funny, sheriff. Ask me about any of the other businesspeople around town and I'll talk for half an hour. I can't make a minute about Hatfield."

"What about our fine district attorney, Jimmy?" Corcoran asked. "We know Phelps was Hatfield's partner. Is there another partner, or someone who might be close enough to almost be considered a partner?"

Henderson sat quietly for a minute looking intently at the tabletop. "Hatfield owed a lot of money to a lot of people, Corcoran. Most did not look on him with favor, certainly not as a partner. He wore out his welcome fast." The saloon owner got contemplative again. "I can't think of anyone."

"Sorry I couldn't get here faster, big boy," Cindy Cook said, flopping down in Corcoran's lap. "Had to take coffee to firefighters and make a hundred thousand sandwiches too."

"You're alone back there?" Sheriff Connor asked. He gave Corcoran a knowing look. "Where's Rosita Chavez?"

"Didn't show up for work. Came in all muddy and I sent her away," Cindy said. "I'm alone back there and this good-looking dude sitting right there," and she pointed at Jimmy Henderson, "is too cheap to hire good help. He's gonna be the death of me," she groaned but with a huge smile on her face. Henderson didn't say a word. He'd heard it all many times.

Corcoran looked at the sheriff. "You were coming down here when we went to Ed Graves's place, sheriff, hoping to run into Wellington or Phelps. Did you?"

"Never made it," Connor said. "Got sidetracked by Mrs. Woodbury. Something about her neighbor's cat or something." He chuckled and looked at Henderson. "Were Wellington and Phelps in here together this evening?"

"Earlier this afternoon but not this evening. Haven't seen either one," Henderson said. He saw a couple of people come in and got up to get behind the bar. "Good luck, you two. Too many fires. Scary."

"He's right about that," Connor said. "Let me read those papers you saved. There might yet be a name in there. It's obvious someone doesn't want this partnership to become public knowledge. Somebody besides Phelps and Wellington will come into a considerable sum of money if that fire insurance is paid."

"If the insurance were to be paid, wouldn't outstanding debt have to be paid before any money is distributed?" Corcoran asked.

Connor's hand froze in place, reaching for the file. "Damn," he said, quietly. "There's going to be another fire, Corcoran. Run as hard as you can run and get Anderson out of his house and away from that bank."

CHAPTER TWENTY

CORCORAN HEARD the muffled *whoomph* of exploding coal oil before he reached the bank. Within seconds, with windows blown out, flames were brilliant in the night sky. "Sumbitch," is all he could say, standing in the middle of the street, staring at the fury inside the building. Jimmy Henderson's words, "too many fires" echoed loud.

With flames from Ed Graves's house shooting thirty feet into the air, and now, smoke pouring from the rock-and-brick Eureka Bank, people were gathering all about once again. "Bring the fire boys," Corcoran shouted at the first to arrive. He raced to Anderson's home and found the front door wide open. He saw the splinters as he went through.

The smell of kerosene attacked his nostrils as he made his way through the large home. *Someone has poured gallons of coal oil but not lit it off. One little spark right now and this whole place goes up. Why wasn't it lit? Why light the bank but not the house unless of course the bastard's still pouring the stuff somewhere else in this house*. Fear strikes men in different ways. Some cringe in terror, some grit their teeth in fear but continue on, and others, those like Terrence Corcoran, face its reality with strength and fortitude.

"Gotta find the bastard before he lights this off," he said. Anderson lived alone and well, and when Corcoran entered the nicely appointed dining room he found two bodies sprawled in puddles of blood and kerosene. The one with the large can of kerosene also had a butcher's knife protruding from his heart. Wellington died hard.

Anderson, too, had a knife in his stomach—a large Bowie-type—stuck deep. *Anderson must have surprised him and paid dearly for the effort. What was Wellington after. Did he get it? Or was he here to kill and destroy.* Corcoran moved the fuel can away from the bodies, despite them already being soaked, and searched through Wellington's pockets.

"So, this is what you wanted, eh?" Corcoran stood over the dead banker with a sheaf of papers that were neatly folded and in an inside frock coat pocket. He looked at Anderson's lifeless hulk. "Are you Connor's third man? Or just protecting your percentage?"

Corcoran was worried about the coal oil being set off but wanted to know where those papers come from. The bank? Anderson's home? He wanted to sit down and read the damn things but knew that would wait. Firefighters, including the chief, came into the room and Corcoran had them move the bodies outside and water the kerosene down before it accidentally got started. "Can you save the bank, chief?"

"Not a chance, Terrence. Not a chance. All that fine

hardwood inside and she's an oven. We won't be able to get close enough to that heat for another ten hours or more. We'll do our best to not let it spread. If it gets too hot, this place will explode too, even with water on all that fuel. What the hell's going on, anyway?"

"I'll let you know as soon as I get it figured out," Corcoran chuckled. "Somebody's trying mighty hard to protect a large sum of money, chief. Lots of money."

"Ain't that always the way? Best get moving, it ain't safe in here."

He held on tight to the papers he took from Anderson and headed to the office. "I could eat a buffalo right now," he muttered, spreading the papers across the sheriff's desk. A full pot of coffee, well laced from Ed Connor's flask, and Corcoran wiped his forehead.

"Mr. Anderson never mentioned any of this, eh? We talked while the Eureka House burned and he never mentioned that he had served papers on Hatfield the day before. He foreclosed on the mortgage and was the owner when it burned. That's why Hatfield put the torch to it, not for the insurance money but to deny Anderson the business. And that's why Hatfield was planning to blow up the bank."

He found several notes and letters he had sent to Hatfield leading up to the foreclosure. *I'd bet a large amount of the county's money that Bill Phelps doesn't know anything about this. How is it that Wellington did?* Corcoran stopped thinking, looked up at the ceiling, and smiled. *He was talking with Ed Graves when Graves was murdered. Graves told him. What a mess. I need to find Phelps and Rosita Chavez and fast.* Corcoran left a note on the sheaf of

papers for Connor and headed out to find the district
attorney and Rosita.

———

CONNOR VISITED the two fire scenes to make sure the
crowds weren't interfering with efforts to contain the
blazes and returned to the office. "Seems we're about ten
minutes late on every fire. Three of the town's largest
buildings, gone. This whole town would be gone right
now if this had been a windy day," he muttered. "I'll pay
my taxes with a smile if those fire boys want more equipment. They have gotten a workout."

Connor read the papers Corcoran left and thumped
the desk several times. "All of this following Maria
Castelleno having a picnic with some guy who murdered
her and we don't have a clue who that might be. Hatfield
ran his business into the ground and borrowed a large
sum from the bank and didn't pay it back and we've got
half a dozen bodies strewn about and a deputy badly
wounded."

He caught himself talking—almost yelling right out
loud—and wagged his head as if in reproach and walked
out the door. "Better check on Mr. Foster instead of
speechifying." The walk on a brisk spring night to Doc
Whidby's gave Connor time to think about the tangled
case.

*Our Mr. Phelps will never hold public office again even if
he's clear of the conspiracy of arson at the Eureka House. I'll see
to that. Mr. Anderson didn't have to die, Maria Castelleno didn't*

have to die, and neither did Ed Graves. The others were outlaws and there's no great loss there.

Connor could be a hard man when he needed to be and simply wrote off the deaths of Hatfield, Sawyer, Wellington, and the others. "I know it's late, Doc, but I wanted to check on our two patients. Lou Foster seemed to be hurt the worst."

"Foster's going to be fine, Ed, but he'll need time to recover. Bullet tore up his shoulder but also broke some bones in there. He lost a lot of blood as well. Your Mr. Bellows can be yours in the morning, but he's got a broken leg to go along with the bullet wound." Whidby gave the sheriff a long look.

"You need some rest, old man. Let Corcoran put the wraps on this mess. He's young, vigorous, and you're a busted up old gent who needs to retire."

"I've heard Corcoran call you a cynical old bastard," Connor laughed. "Now I know why. Where did you get most of your training? You know, like bedside manner?"

"The war, Ed." He rarely talked about those terrible times. Whidby was still in training—young, willing, and able when the war broke out. He volunteered for medical service immediately and no one got trained faster than he.

"That horrible two-headed war. First war was ending slavery, man's inhumanity to man, and the second, the cruelty of men killing men, brother killing brother. Hideous wounds, horrible and terrible pressures driving men mad. I learned my skills standing for days on end at the surgery table, covered in other men's blood, cutting away limbs, watching in horror as the bodies were stacked five and six deep."

Whidby stood, shoulders slumped, resting against the door jamb. His sad eyes looked Connor up and down. "I guess I am just a cynical old doctor, sheriff."

"I don't think you're as cynical as you are a profound and deep-thinking man, Doc. Eureka County is lucky to have a man like you caring for us." He reached out and squeezed his old friend's shoulder and smiled. "And I think you're right. I probably should retire after this term. Got two more years to go and with Corcoran as my chief deputy, I'll make it fine. Is Foster awake?"

"No. I've got 'em both doped up pretty good. Come back in the morning, Ed. Go home and sleep. Dream good thoughts of you and me hunting elk later this year or fishing with those English fly rods I have coming in. Go home."

CORCORAN MADE his way through town and down into the gulch on the north side, toward Bill Phelps's home. *It's just me again. Sheriff's gettin' old, tries too hard, but we all reach that point, I guess. New deputy's all shot up. Insurance investigators are interesting—one's dead, working against me and the other's shot up, working for me. Phelps gives me any back talk and I'll send him off to the promised land in a hurry.*

He had to chuckle at the thought, walking along the dark street at the bottom of the gulch. He stiffened up realizing what a target he was. Anyone could be standing in the dark shadows and blow his head off and he'd never see it coming. Corcoran moved to the darkest side of the roadway, deep in the shadows and moved slowly toward the DA's home. *Sometimes I think I deserve to be shot by some idiot. Get your mind back on business, old man.*

He saw trees, or were they men with rifles? He saw bushes, but they could be a man all hunched over with a Colt cocked and ready. He also saw looming shadows, any one of which could hide half a squad of angry men looking to kill him. Walking the streets late at night, no moon, houses darkened, is a frightful thing even for a deputy sheriff primed for action.

He was as alert as a man could be, trying to watch both sides of the road at the same time. Large trees, cottonwood, fruit trees, some pines and spruce, made for interesting shadows, any of which could hide a person with a gun. He was across the narrow street from the Phelps' place and was surprised to not see light shining from any of the windows.

"It ain't that late," he muttered. He stood quiet thinking what he would be doing if he was in Bill Phelps's situation. Did Phelps even know that the bank was the owner of the Eureka House when it burned? Did Hatfield tell him? Did Wellington find out from Ed Graves? Was Wellington involved? "Well, yes," he muttered. "Wellington knew since he murdered the banker but when did he find out?"

Corcoran caught the slightest movement off to his right, almost toward the rear of the Phelps' place. *That ain't a dog or a horse, old man. Let's just watch for a minute.* The shadowy figure moved cautiously from tree to tree across the yard. *That's the muddy yard where we found the boots and prints.*

Corcoran used as much of the shadows as he could and slipped across the roadway. There was a low hedge and he got down as low as possible, following the hedge toward the figure, now standing behind a pine tree. *Just another twenty feet.* There was no moon, few clouds, but the starlight wasn't enough for Corcoran to identify the figure. *Ain't very big. Another ten feet and I've got him.* Someone lurking in the backyard of a darkened home was suspicious by itself, but when that home belonged to a murder and arson suspect, Corcoran wanted to know all there was to know.

Corcoran was at the end of the hedge and knew the figure was looking toward the house from behind the tree. *Get more behind that tree and I've got you. Come on, get behind the tree.* It was too far to rush and not get shot doing it and Corcoran wanted this person alive and able to talk. Corcoran pulled his revolver and the shadowy figure moved behind the tree.

He rushed the two yards and slammed the revolver into the person's head. "Oh my god," he said, catching the unconscious body of Rosita Chavez. A second person emerged from the dark, swung a rifle, driving the barrel end hard into Corcoran's head.

CHAPTER TWENTY-ONE

"BRING HIM IN HERE, boys. Right on the table there," Doctor Whidby said. "This is getting out of line. Where'd you find him?"

Corcoran's scalp was ripped open, bleeding profusely, and swollen from the smashing blows. His deep-red hair was covered in mud, blood, and yard debris. "He was spread-eagle in the middle of the road down in the gulch. We almost drove the team right over him," Pete Hutchins said. "Somebody don't like him from the looks of that head. Whopped him more than once."

"Thanks, boys. I'll take care of him." Whidby was surprised seeing Corcoran's belt holster empty. "Where's his gun?"

"Didn't have one in his holster. Gonna be raining soon, Doc. Gotta get this stuff up to the store," Hutchins said. Hutchins' Grocery was known for its fresh vegetables and yard-raised chicken, duck, goose, and rabbit meat. Pete and Will Hutchins and their wives were a busy bunch. The two families had a passel of kids to keep the weeds down.

"Well, Mr. Corcoran, let's see what I can do to make you feel better." Corcoran had not regained consciousness as Doc Whidby began cleaning his wounds. "Whoever hit you was a big man to cause this much damage. Not like you to not shoot him first. Hit you right straight on, too, not like he snuck up from behind. How did that happen, Corcoran?"

Whidby carried on a complete one-sided conversation with Terrence as he cleaned and sutured the ugly wound. "You're gonna hurt bad, my friend. That will make you one dangerous man. God help the man that whupped on your head." He went to Art Bellows's bed and got him awake.

"Corcoran's been hurt. Sit with him while I find the sheriff, will you? If he wakes up before I get back, try to keep him under control. He might very well have a concussion and not be thinking straight. He'll need his rest, but I do know the gentleman better than that."

Bellows chuckled and hobbled on his one good leg and a crutch, his broken leg wrapped tight in a cast, to where Corcoran was stretched out. "He looks like a peaceful man when he's sleeping, Doc."

"He isn't," Whidby said. He found his coat and hat and slipped out the door.

"Doc said you were found down in the gulch, eh? Were you anywhere near Bill Phelps's place? And who did you find?" He was talking to an unconscious man, he thought, and was surprised when Corcoran answered him.

"Rosita Chavez," Corcoran mumbled. "Thought she was alone."

"Catch a glimpse of whoever smashed that ugly head of yours?" Bellows asked.

"Just a shadow of a large man." He coughed, groaned from the pain of it, tried to sit up and couldn't. "Your partner's dead, Art." Bellows let out a strong breath and Corcoran could see the man tense up.

"Tried to kill the banker. Actually, did kill the banker, but Mr. Anderson killed Wellington too. The bank's just cinders now. Listen to me, now. Things are getting fuzzy, can't seem to focus my eyes or my thinking. Don't let me pass out, Bellows. This is important."

"I'm with you, Corcoran." Bellows found a water jug and filled a glass. "Drink some of this. Doc Whidby says you probably have a concussion. You took a hell of a blow to the head, my friend. What was Wellington doing at the bankers?"

"He burned the bank down and went to Anderson's home to kill the man. Listen now." Corcoran tried to shake his head, as if shaking off the thick clouds getting in the way of his thinking. "Anderson foreclosed on the Eureka House property the day before Hatfield burned it down. Phelps doesn't own nothing." Corcoran said and Bellows almost gasped.

"Amazing," Bellows said. He walked around the bed, wagged his head back and forth, and finally just sat down on the edge of the bed. "That really changes this entire situation, Corcoran. Does Phelps know that?"

"I doubt it. Don't know how it came to be that Wellington knew. Probably from Graves just before he was killed. The bank owns the property. I've got it all in writing at the office. How is it that Wellington seemed to know that?" Corcoran's mind didn't seem to grasp what he already knew. Graves told him. He drank the water and made a funny face. "Thought you handed me whiskey."

Bellows was stunned at this turn of events and stood back up at the side of Corcoran's bed, staring out at the wall in front of him. "I don't know," he murmured. "Wellington was very secretive with anything he knew about a property. Apparently, Phelps didn't know either. He would have said something when we were there."

"I have an idea, but it's just a thought," Corcoran said. "What if Wellington went to the bank after it closed to find out what Anderson knew of the partnerships and discovered the foreclosure papers. It would have cut him out of whatever percentage Phelps had offered him. Furious, he left, came back with the kerosene to burn out the bank and the records and then kill and burn down Anderson's home."

"Sure makes sense to me," Bellows said. "Leaves Mr. Phelps with nothing. He was a partner in a business that had just been foreclosed on. Would make for an upset and angry man. Angry enough to bash in your head, I'm thinking."

Corcoran shook his wounded head slowly. "No, Graves told him. He went to the bank to find the papers and couldn't. Angry, he burned the bank and headed for Anderson's. Anderson had the foreclosure papers in his pocket, the two fought and died."

Bellows started to say something, and Corcoran cut

him off. "I'm not an attorney so I'm just speculating here, but in my mind right now, even though Anderson is dead, the bank owns that property, and if Hatfield set it on fire he burned down something he didn't own. Would that mean the insurance, despite the arson, would be paid off?"

"Probably," Bellows said. "You think it was Phelps that hit you? Couldn't have been either Wellington or Anderson."

"If it was Bill Phelps who did it, then he and Rosita might have been planning something. The house was dark, and it was her moving around in the dark backyard that brought me in. I smashed her in the head with my gun not knowing it was her. That's when I got knocked around."

"Walked right into it, eh?" Bellows didn't chuckle or snicker, just stood their shaking his head some. "Doc Whidby went to get the sheriff, Corcoran. I think it might be the right time for me to take a look at what might be going on at Phelps's place. Tell the sheriff he's welcome to join me when he gets here."

Bellows headed out and Corcoran lay his head back on the pillow. He was asleep that fast. Art Bellows was a strong man and even so found it difficult to make his way through the late night, very early morning dark to the Phelps' home. The rain as predicted by the grocery brothers was just starting and the crutches didn't always behave themselves in the mud. Bellows stood in the deep shadows across the street and unlike when Corcoran had been there, he could see light coming from burning lamps inside.

"Phelps is probably nursing Rosita's bashed-in head. Sure would like to hear that conversation." Bellows fought his way across the street, stayed in the shadows as he made his way to a window and crept as close as he dared. "I think if I had a place like this I'd have a dog. A big one," he murmured.

There was a thorny rosebush in front of the window and Bellows had to get almost into it to get close enough to see or hear anything. "Stickers, damn it." He saw Phelps on his knees in front of a couch where Rosita Chavez was stretched out. Her head was as much a bloody mess as Corcoran's had been. Phelps was saying something, but Bellows couldn't make out what.

Rosita was wearing muddy boots and Bellows took a quick look at Phelps. *It had to be Phelps who whacked Corcoran by the looks of those boots. I wonder what they were doing out there? He said the house was dark and neither one had a lamp. I think I better have a look around.*

Rain was falling a little stronger as morning light slowly took over from the shades of night. Bellows found a shovel and pick leaning against the tree that Rosita was standing behind and a small plot of freshly dug-up ground. *They buried something or were about to? Doc Whidby said Corcoran looked like he was hit with a rifle barrel. I wonder if it wasn't a shovel?*

Phelps had a small carriage house tucked away behind his house off to the side of this small yard and Bellows carefully made his way to it. It was getting light fast, and the rain was now being driven by strong gusty winds. He could hear water rushing down the creek at the bottom of the gulch and ducked behind a large willow when he saw the back door of the house coming open.

Phelps, alone and not in heavy outerwear, made a dash to the carriage house, leaving the door to the house open. *If Corcoran was with me right now, I'd take Phelps and he'd make a run for the house. Gonna have to let this play out, I guess.* The area from the willow tree to the back porch or to the carriage house was open, no place to hide, and Bellows simply stood in the rain and waited.

It was just minutes and Phelps came out, looked around the yard quickly, and made a dash for the back door. He held a small box that appeared to be rather heavy. Bellows waited for just moments and made his way to the carriage house, slipping in as quietly as he could. The rain pounded on the roof of the building and Bellows chuckled. *As if someone could have heard me run over here.*

Several windows allowed considerable light into the building and Bellows stood still, letting his eyes slowly search out what might have brought Phelps out in this weather. "I'll be damned," he said. He skirted around a small corral holding a bay mare, who snickered at him, and stood in front of an open safe. Several filled and tied-off canvas bags were evident along with a second box similar to what Phelps carried into the house.

Leaving it open like this means he's coming back for more. Bellows looked about some more, saw a small carriage with harness hung nearby for the mare, garden tools, and a few items Phelps would use in caring for his horse. The small barn was neat—items and tools cared for and stored away, ready for use.

How long before the big man comes back? Was he armed? Questions flooded Bellows's thoughts as he tried to kneel in front of the small vault. His leg in a cast made the move more than complicated and he found he was on one knee with his broken leg stretched out to the side. He untied one of the canvas bags. It was filled with twenty-dollar gold coins. *Bags full of double eagles. Hatfield's saloon and hotel was foreclosed on the day before it burned to the ground because he didn't pay the bank's loan, yet his partner has bags full of double eagles.*

The next thought was something about Hatfield also having had bags full of double eagles. "They were skimming their own business," Bellows murmured. "Where would Hatfield's share be? At that old barn?" He remembered Corcoran saying that the arsonists were paid five thousand dollars for their end of the job.

I've got to get out of here before that fool comes back for more gold. Bellows started for the door and heard the back door of the house open up, heard heavy footfalls splashing across the yard and despite his leg in a cast, managed to crawl under the small carriage without being seen or heard.

Phelps came in, again without rainwear, and walked straight to the safe and picked up the second box. He looked around the building, as if he smelled or maybe saw something, stood quietly for just a moment, shrugged his shoulders, and walked out the door. Bellows didn't wait. He almost followed Phelps to the door and waited for the big man to dash across the yard and close the back door. "Did they bury gold? Or," and he wagged his head some, "is this what they were digging up? I need some help down here and I need it fast."

A hundred questions rushed through his mind as he made his way across the now very well-lit backyard and on up the street to the sheriff's office. *There had to have been thousands of dollars in those boxes and bags. How much more didn't I see? If Hatfield and Phelps were able to skim this much money off the property, that tells me the property would have actually been making money. None of this was necessary.*

It was three blocks, two of them uphill, on crutches, while mother nature threw a fit. The rains came as predicted, in blinding sheets, driven by gale-force winds. His crutches slipped in the mud, stuck in the clay, and wallowed in the gravel accompanied by some of the foulest language ever heard in central Nevada, but insurance investigator Arthur Bellows managed to make it to the sheriff's warm and dry office.

CHAPTER TWENTY-TWO

"You look like a drowned rat, Mr. Bellows." Sheriff Ed Connor laughed as the insurance investigator almost tripped coming through the door.

"It's bad enough having to negotiate this village in a cast and using crutches, you've brought on Noah's inundations as well," the big man stormed. "My heavens, sheriff, the water in your main street is deep enough for a steamship, I'm sure."

"Here, get out of that huge coat and stand by the fire. Where have you been?"

"I've been at Phelps's place, sheriff. I thought you were going to join me? I left word with Corcoran to tell you my plans."

"Corcoran was unconscious, Mr. Bellows. Never got a chance to talk to him. You look like there's some more you want to say." Connor poured the two some coffee and pulled that almost always full flask from the bottom drawer. "Let's talk, eh?"

"Corcoran said he left some papers on the desk for you. Have you read them? What I'm going to say probably fits right in somehow."

Connor pointed to the sheaf and nodded. "The most interesting thing I've read in years, Mr. Bellows. We have to believe that Phelps didn't know about this. It's logical, though, that Hatfield did know his business had been foreclosed on." The sheriff stopped and contemplated what he just said. "Why burn it, then?"

Bellows threw more wood in the already hot stove, poured more coffee, and got as close to the stove as a man could without catching his clothing on fire. "That rain is cold, sheriff. As far as I know, Phelps was not aware, but on the other hand, my partner, Wellington, may have been. Don't know why he would, though. Interesting, eh?"

"I'm thinking that Ed Graves told him just before he was shot to death. Graves would have been the one to tell Hatfield as well," the sheriff said.

Bellows pulled a chair over and sat down. For the next ten minutes he described what took place at Phelps's home—the freshly dug hole, the bags and boxes of gold, and the availability of a horse and carriage. "My biggest question right now concerns that digging," Bellows said. "Did they dig up the gold or were they getting ready to bury it? If they dug it up, are they planning to run off? And if they were about to bury it, why?"

Ed Connor was a thinking man and he put together half a dozen possibilities as Bellows talked. Yes, Phelps could run off but that wasn't his style. Bury the gold? Or did he dig it up? Was the digging related to the gold at all? "We'll have to tackle this as if it were a crime," the sheriff said. "It might be, you know." Connor poured some whiskey in his tin cup, ignoring the coffee pot, and sat back in his swivel rocker.

"Why is Rosita involved in this? She was planning to scam old man Castelleno out of his mine and property. Supposedly hated Phelps and Hatfield for their messing around with Maria Castelleno." Connor sat forward some and picked up the foreclosure papers, looked them over carefully and put them back down.

"Mr. Phelps became district attorney after representing Castelleno as a private attorney in several actions. He gained quite a reputation from that," Connor said. "Probably when he started his meetings with Maria and probably when he became partners with Gordon Hatfield. You following me, Mr. Bellows?"

"I am, sheriff, but not sure where you're leading us."

"Neither am I, sir," Connor chuckled. "My biggest question is still this. How does Rosita Chavez fit into this situation? We have been led to believe that she hated Hatfield and Phelps for their offensive behavior with Mrs. Castelleno. Why is she so close to Phelps?"

"You'll not get an answer from me," Bellows said. "Did Doc Whidby give you any idea when Corcoran will be back on his feet? We need that man right now."

"We won't have him for a day or two, Mr. Bellows. Let's go get some breakfast and keep talking. We're both good thinkers. We can figure this out."

Bellows leg hurt like hell, he was still wet despite being almost cuddled up to the stove and didn't want to go. The sheriff was in his coat and out the door before

Bellows could say anything and finally got in his coat and hobbled along, well behind Connor. Swirling rain laced with ice crystals that felt like needles peppered his face as he lurched across the main street.

"Can't even see across the street. No feelings," Bellows muttered. "The man simply has no feelings for his fellow man." The muttering continued all the way across the main street and into the Bonanza Club, half filled with sopping wet men standing at the bar, dripping, in some cases steaming, and drinking heartily.

"What's brought this on, sheriff? Almost a party atmosphere in here," Bellows said, trying his best to protect his broken leg from those moving about.

"The rain, Mr. Bellows. They can't or won't work in this maelstrom, but they know it will make everything grow and they'll have good herds, good grass, and good crops this year. Yes, it is a party atmosphere." Connor waved and caught Cindy Cook's attention and she in turn pointed them out to Jimmy Henderson behind the bar.

"Assuming Phelps was stealing money from the Eureka House operation, and that Hatfield was probably doing the same, the answer has to be why? Obviously with that much money being raked off the top, the saloon-hotel was making money. Why not just pay the mortgage and take their shares?"

Connor didn't know and the look Bellows gave him was a sign the insurance investigator didn't either. "There has to be a third person who was being cut out. If it was Anderson at the bank, he foreclosed but will not receive full measure," Bellows said. "I'm thinking there is a third partner who was being cut out."

"It would have been even more secret than Phelps's partnership. No other name was on the foreclosure papers or mortgage," Connor said. "Well, well, look who's up and about."

Connor stood up and pulled a chair back for Lou Foster who looked like any of the other drowned rats infesting the Bonanza, except he had a few more bandages showing. "Feeling well enough to be out, are you?"

"Had to get out of there. Felt all caged up," Foster said. "Me and Corcoran been talking about the foreclosure papers he found. He wanted me to find you and give you our thoughts."

"That's why we're here, Lou," Connor said. "Have breakfast with us and tell us all about it because we haven't come up with any answers."

Foster looked at the two filling their coffee cups half full of whiskey and shook his head. "It ain't early for us, young 'un," Connor growled it out and Foster knew he'd never make that mistake again. "Been workin' all night. Tell us what you and Corcoran come up with."

"Well, sheriff," Foster almost stammered. "Corcoran thinks there's a third person we don't know about, and he thinks it might even be Alphonso Castelleno himself. He seems to think that Castelleno and Phelps were the ones who helped fund Gordon Hatfield in the first place."

"Oh, my," Bellows said. "There's no money out at that barn that Hatfield was so proud of, sheriff. Phelps and Castelleno were ripping off Hatfield." He leaned way back in his chair and roared with laughter, catching the attention of many around their table.

"There's more," Foster said. Bellows had a hard time stopping his laughter and Connor finally rapped the table with his knuckles to get things calmed down.

"Go ahead, Lou. You already stomped on us with that first one," Bellows said. "It makes perfect sense, though. Castelleno and Phelps had already worked hard together on court cases. Phelps was never one to be considered clean and tidy with his interpretation of the law. What else has Corcoran come up with?"

"Rosita Chavez," Foster said. Connor and Bellows looked at each other, questions in their eyes. "He thinks the lady may be in serious danger. If Castelleno and Phelps are partnered up, she has already told Phelps of her plans to poison the old mine owner. Phelps may have more connection with Castelleno because of money than he has with Rosita because of bedtime pleasures."

"This Phelps character has a lot on his plate, sheriff. He was playing house with Maria Castelleno while partnering up with her husband. And Maria ended up dead, sheriff. Now, he's playing house with the woman who has said right out that she plans to murder the mine owner. I think Corcoran's right. Rosita Chavez's life is in danger."

"I agree," Connor said. "That might also name Bill Phelps as Maria's murderer." He took a long drink of whiskey forgetting there was no coffee in the cup, coughed hard, wiped his eyes, and had an ironic smile across his face when he looked at Lou Foster.

"Here's the deal," Connor said, getting his mind back on track. "Mr. Bellows, you get yourself back up to Doc's and get head-to-head with Corcoran. You, Mr. Foster, you come with me as we visit Mr. Phelps. All right, now. Eat fast and we'll save a life or two," he chuckled.

Cindy Cook had platters of pork chops, mashed potatoes, bowls of gravy, and another pot of coffee at the table. "Biscuits will be coming right out of the oven in another couple of minutes, fellows. Eat hearty."

CHAPTER TWENTY-THREE

"CAN'T REMEMBER when it rained this hard, Foster," Ed Connor said as they sloshed their way down along the gulch road. Sometimes the spring rains drift along on warm breezes and other times they are the mad hatters of the atmosphere—not dancing, but whirling as the dervishes would. It was that kind of morning the two were moving through.

"Just look at that creek. Roiled, I'd say." Connor pointed out the crashing of the creek along the canyon bottom.

"Won't be fishin' for a while," Foster chuckled. "What was Bellows talking about gold and Phelps digging in his backyard?"

Connor told him about Bellows's trip to the Phelps' place earlier that morning. "He saw thousands of dollars in gold coins, Lou. When we get to the house, I want you to stand back a ways and keep an eye on the back of the house if you can. I'm going right up to the front door.

Bellows said there is a horse and carriage so somebody might try to make a run for it."

Foster moved over to the creek side of the road, then the house side of the road and stopped along a hedgerow. The back of the house sloped down slightly to the carriage house and behind that, down just a bit, was the creek. "Another couple of hours of this rain and the creek'll overflow its banks for sure," the young deputy murmured.

He stood near the hedge, could see Connor walking up the walkway to the front door and could plainly see the backyard and carriage house. The rain was incessant, driven by strong winds, and carried the remnants of winter's cold. "Reminds me of sitting on the back of a fine horse trying to keep the cows from drowning. Nobody ever gave a damn if one of us drowned." He shook his head remembering the cow boss saying something like, 'Just sing to 'em. Makes you feel better.' "I ain't singing, sheriff," he muttered.

Connor banged on the door and stood slightly off to the side. Phelps opened the door and called the sheriff in. Connor was surprised to see the large man in a housecoat and slippers.

"Not feeling well, Mr. Phelps? Understandable with this weather," Connor said. *Most interesting. Bellows said he was fully dressed and in heavy rain gear earlier.* "Have a couple of questions that need answering, sir. It's come to light that Gordon Hatfield was served certain papers the day before he allegedly burned his Eureka House business to the ground."

"Papers, sheriff? What kind of papers?" Phelps sat

down, heavily, in one of the couches in the living room. Connor couldn't help notice the bloody rags still evident, probably from when he cleaned up Rosita's banged-up head. Or did they come from something a little more recent?

"The Eureka Bank served foreclosure papers on the business, Mr. Phelps. Surely, as a partner, you would have been informed." Phelps sucked in air and sat bolt upright with his mouth open. Connor realized the man knew nothing about the foreclosure and that this had come as a complete surprise. "Your partner didn't bother to tell you?"

Phelps sat on the couch, his mouth open as if to say something, but didn't. He shook his head, glared at the sheriff, wanted to say something and had no idea what to say. "Come now, Mr. Phelps, you and Hatfield were close, weren't you? Business partners? Partners in enjoying the company of Maria Castelleno, eh?" Connor was pushing hard and not getting the kind of reaction he had hoped for. Phelps just looked at him. Any other man would have drawn a weapon and shot the sheriff.

"Foreclosed?" Phelps muttered. "Anderson foreclosed? I don't understand," Phelps said. He was deflated—just a sack of flesh, fat and bone sitting on the couch, rocking back and forth. "The insurance?"

"If it weren't for the arson, sir, it would be paid to the owner of the business, Mr. Phelps. That would be the Eureka Bank. How are you going to tell your other partner? Will you warn him of Miss Chavez's plans to kill him?"

"How did..." Phelps didn't finish the question and

Connor did his best to hold off a grand smile. Connor's first thought was, gotcha, but he didn't let up. He had Phelps dancing on thin strings and needed to come to the end of the play. "While we're on the subject, Mr. Phelps, exactly where is Rosita Chavez? We know she was here earlier this morning or late last night. We know you doctored her head after Corcoran smashed it."

Phelps just sat on the couch, quiet, staring at the rug under his slippered feet. His world was crashing in around him. He had done so well, he and Castelleno, taking all that gold regularly from the business. Phelps insisted on doing the accounting and took pride in showing Hatfield the doctored ledgers. Hatfield was such a lame, egotistical fool that, since his partner was the district attorney, he figured he would never rip him off.

It's all gone, just like that. Thousands of dollars in hoarded gold coins and then we were going to get the insurance money from the fire, and I could be free from this miserable hole of a village, live in San Francisco, dress in finery that isn't covered in mud. Phelps was so sure he had things covered, that he and Castelleno were in the clear. *How has this happened?*

He looked up at Sheriff Ed Connor standing over him. Connor thought he had never seen such sad eyes in all his years of arresting crooks, murderers, and con men. "Where is Rosita Chavez, Mr. Phelps? I need to speak with her."

"She left several hours ago, sheriff. Went back to the mine and Mr. Castelleno. What did you mean that she would kill the old man?"

It was Connor's turn to be brought up short. "You

didn't know?" He asked and paced around a little bit. "Damn."

This was awkward, Connor thought. Phelps was involved in a multi-headed conspiracy that he might not have any active part in. *My God, this man can't even be arrested at this point,* he almost thought out loud.

After all, he reasoned, it wasn't Phelps who arranged for the Eureka House to burn down. It wasn't Phelps who killed Ed Graves. Phelps didn't kill Gordon Hatfield. Phelps may have taken money from his partner, but Hatfield didn't bring charges.

Connor's mind was spinning. *There's no crime here that I can pin on Bill Phelps.* Connor forgot that it was probably Phelps and Rosita who had done the shooting when Corcoran, Bellow, and Foster were in the Graves's house. "Did Miss Chavez take the horse and carriage out back?"

"No, she walked up to the Bonanza to get someone to drive her out to the mine. She was going to have a face-to-face meeting with Castelleno. He still owed her money. I'm sure she won't come back here."

"Oh? And, why would that be?" *She never told Phelps she was going to get back in good standing with Castelleno, marry him, and poison the old man? He might be an attorney, but this man is one big fool.* "Come now, Phelps. Why?"

"My wife will be home on tomorrow's train, sheriff. I won't see Rosita again." Phelps sat absolutely still, staring at the floor, not shaking in fear, not sobbing, just sitting with his head between his legs, subdued and quiet.

"Thank you," Connor said and slipped into his heavy gear. "We'll have another chat, soon, I'm sure." He walked out of the house and found Lou Foster, still standing near the hedge, drenched, shivering, maybe just a bit angry. "Let's get back to the office, Mr. Foster. We have quite a bit to talk about."

———

BELLOWS, Corcoran, and Doctor Whidby were gathered around the stove in the sheriff's office when they arrived, dripping wet, cold, and, as Foster said later, the sheriff was grouchy. "What are you doing out of bed?" Connor stormed at Corcoran.

"Same question I want an answer for," Whidby said.

"My head hurts but I'm fine," Corcoran said. Whidby just harrumphed some and turned away. Corcoran gave that little boy grin of his and continued. "What did you find out at Phelps's? Any bodies show up?"

Connor outlined what he learned and sat at his desk. He was a dejected man. "Can't arrest the fool. It isn't illegal to be stupid. He's involved up to his crooked neck in a bunch of dead people, in the burning of three or four buildings, in injured deputies, and hasn't broken one single law that I can think of." He slammed his hand onto the desktop and immediately reached for the third drawer down on the left side.

"He slammed that rifle across the side of my head," Corcoran said. "As far as I can remember, that is a crime."

"It is, but there isn't anyone around these parts that saw him do it," Connor barked.

"You said Rosita went to the Bonanza to find a ride out to the mine," Corcoran said, looking back and forth from Connor to Foster. "You were there. Did either of you see her? Did anyone say anything? Her injuries have to be obvious. Someone would have seen."

Bellows, Foster, and Connor looked at each other and shook their heads. "Cindy would have said something if she had seen her," Connor said. "I should have demanded that I search Phelps's place before I left. Damn fool stunt not to have. Think her body's stuffed in a hole?"

"Maybe that big bay and carriage aren't really there, sheriff," Corcoran said. "Phelps's reaction when you all but said that he and Castelleno were partners proved the point?" Connor nodded and Corcoran continued. "And Rosita supposedly didn't tell Phelps about her plans to marry Castelleno? I wonder why?"

"Rosita is on her way out there and Castelleno is in trouble," Bellows said. He looked around the small office and said, ever so quietly, "I can't ride with a cast on my leg." Corcoran held his head and smiled, and Connor started moving papers around on his desk.

Lou Foster groaned.

CHAPTER TWENTY-FOUR

IF IT COULD HAVE BEEN SEEN, the sun would have been climbing toward its zenith as Lou Foster rode his cow pony slowly through sheets of cold, wind-driven rain toward the Castelleno Mine. He could almost see the wind and watched the currents drive thousands of gallons of water in undulating waves. "It would be pretty if I wasn't the target," he murmured. His mumbling would have many more curse words than slang, and there would have been no soft singing as to a bedded herd.

"The worst part, Horse," he said, "I begged for this job." He was wearing a wool shirt covered with a heavy wool coat, which in turn was covered by his slicker. Despite all that, Lou Foster was cold and wet as he stepped down from Horse and made his way through the mud to Castelleno's front door.

The young boy answered the door and escorted Foster into the great room. Alphonso Castelleno and Rosita Chavez were seated in front of the fireplace and the old man rose to welcome the young deputy. Foster was surprised to find the woman there. Her head was wrapped in bandages stained with blood, her eyes, one had been bruised before Corcoran slammed her with his long-barreled Colt, were so purple they were black.

"These visits from the sheriff's office are becoming unwelcome. Just what is it you want this time?" Castelleno asked.

"I'd like a few moments alone with you, sir," Foster said. *The sheriff didn't say what to say if Rosita was here. Sure can't warn the old man with her sitting right there. What would Corcoran do?*

"Anything you have to say to me can be said in front of the lady," Castelleno said. "We have no secrets between us." He smiled down at Rosita who returned the offering. "I've been an old fool and chastised this fine friend for wanting to help me when my late wife betrayed our marriage. She's a shining example of what a true friend is."

Foster wanted to shuck the slicker and stand near the fire, knew he needed to warn Castelleno of the threat from Rosita Chavez, and found he could do none of that. "The sheriff was insistent that we talk alone, sir," Foster said. "The message I brought is very personal, sir."

"Nothing is personal between Miss Chavez and me," Castelleno said. "We'll be husband and wife within the day, deputy. Say what you have to say."

"No, I'm afraid I can't," Foster said. "Excuse the visit." He turned and walked out of the room and noticed that Castelleno did not try to stop him. *Ain't this just a pile of corral stuff. He's gonna do what I was sent out to warn him not to do.* "Well, Horse, let's ride on back, enjoy this wonderful spring day, and try not to drown." It took just a moment or two for him to see the carriage standing at the far rail, hitched to a fine bay.

———

"THE MAN IS OBSTINATE," Corcoran said when Foster came back and told his story. "It's hard to warn someone who doesn't want to be warned. What do we do about Mr. Phelps? The sheriff was right in his thinking. He hasn't killed anyone, hasn't burned any buildings down, didn't try to rob the bank. And to the best of my knowledge was not the man who killed Maria Castelleno."

Corcoran, sitting behind the sheriff's desk held his cup out for Foster to fill it up. "On the other hand, being involved in a conspiracy to have people killed, to have buildings burned down, to be involved in other crimes is against the law, Mr. Foster. Let's you and I go visit Mr. Phelps, eh?"

Foster didn't even have the energy to groan this time, just grabbed his wool jacket, heavy with rainwater, his slicker, and followed Corcoran out into the roaring tempest. "You sure you're up to this?" he asked, maybe hoping Corcoran would change his mind. Not a chance.

Corcoran wore an old capote he'd had for years. The hood covered his heavily bandaged head since he couldn't wear his sombrero. "You look like an old mountain man," Foster joshed as they made their way down to the gulch road. "Think Phelps will even be there?"

"He will. He'll also be angry as a mule when he finds out his horse and carriage are gone. He has a lot of gold to move somewhere safe before his wife gets home. I'm sure she's not in his plans. Never will understand why some men marry the women they hole up with."

"Ain't gonna get married, myself," Foster said. "My pa had a good woman. I'd marry someone like my mother but ain't never found one even close. Why ain't you married, Corcoran?"

"Came mighty close, once. A long time ago, Lou. Ain't never found one like Crazy Hair since." He stopped short, peering out into the sheeting rain toward Phelps's house. "Ain't that Phelps leaving his porch?"

"Sure is," Foster said.

"Wherever he's going, we'll just follow along. Stay back and try to not make enough noise to catch his attention. Probably going for a nice springtime walk and an afternoon drink or two at the Bonanza Club."

"That's good," Foster chuckled. "That's where the sheriff and Mr. Bellows are."

It was an easy two-block walk through an angry storm back up to the main street but Phelps turned into the telegraph office, not the saloon. "We'll get up on the boardwalk and under the overhang, there, Foster. Wonder who he's sending a wire to?"

"Or getting one?" Foster asked and saw Corcoran's face light up just a bit.

"Good thinking, Lou." *He's gonna be a good man to carry a badge. Why is Phelps in the telegraph office? Most interesting.*

Phelps wasn't there but five minutes and headed off to the saloon. "Stay with him and join up with Connor and Bellows. I'll be along shortly," Corcoran said. He watched Lou follow off and stepped into the office. "Howdy, Lem, think this rain'll ever stop?"

"Humboldt River is already over its banks in Winnemucca, Terrence. Humboldt Sink will be full this year. What can I do for you?" Lem Phillips had been with the telegraph company since it came to Eureka.

"Sheriff business, I'm afraid. What was Phelps doing?"

"Oh no, Terrence. You know better. You of all people. You gotta have a warrant from the judge."

"Well, that's true but you can tell me whether he sent a wire or whether he got one. That you can do."

"Ain't supposed to, but I will. His wife's due in tomorrow and he sent her a wire telling her about this horrible weather and told her to stay in Virginia City for another day or two. I wish you wouldn't force me to do these things, Terrence," Lem Phillips said. He didn't do a very good job of holding in a chuckle.

"Not a word about this," Corcoran said, and walked out, back into the rain to the Bonanza Club. *He's gonna get that gold in a small wagon, find a good team, and flee the scene, sure as I'm Corcoran, Terrence Corcoran. I doubt that he'll leave until this storm passes, though. Those roads out there have to be all but impassable. Have to be. Where oh where would he get a good team and wagon? I'll head up to Afeldt's livery in a while.*

———

FOSTER FOLLOWED Phelps and was surprised when the man turned up toward Abe Afeldt's blacksmith shop. "Damn," he muttered. "Corcoran won't know this. He was sure the man was heading for the saloon." The wind and rain hadn't let up a bit since early that morning and Foster was sure the storm was getting even stronger as he neared the blacksmith's.

Foster couldn't find a single place to get in out of the rain and still see Afeldt's place. *I can't just stand out in the storm like a damn fool. Can't walk in and say howdy either.* He wasted less than a minute on the problem and headed quickly down to the main street and into the Bonanza Club.

"Phelps is at Afeldt's, Corcoran. No place to hide so came here to tell you."

"That's fine, Lou. Just fine. Afeldt's, eh? Lost his horse and carriage and looking for a replacement, I'd wager." He looked over at Ed Connor and Art Bellows. "Damn close to what I just outlined, gentlemen. He's gonna run."

"I can't stop him, or if he did run, he would become a wanted man," Bellows said. "I'm going to find the justice of the peace, get a hearing date set, and see if I can get orders to force witnesses to stay in town. It's worked before," he said.

Tommy Trimble was in his office when Bellows and Corcoran slopped their way in. "I'm gonna need a drainage ditch right here in the office if this storm keeps up," Trimble joshed. "Just hang the wet stuff on the hooks. You're not the first to come in sopping wet today."

"We have an interesting request, Tommy," Corcoran said. "You set day after tomorrow for the hearing on the Eureka House insurance claim. Some of the people who were going to be witnesses are now dead, I'm worried that others might try to run away, leave town."

"In this weather?" Trimble laughed and pointed out the window.

"Dangerous men do stupid things, Your Honor," Bellows said. "There have been a lot of people die in these last few weeks. There have been some serious changes to what would have been a difficult hearing to start with. Some of those who will be testifying may just want to skip town."

Bellows and Corcoran knew better than to single out Phelps and instead were more than general in their observations. Trimble was a fast thinker and saw what they were doing. "Do you have more than one person in mind, here?" he asked.

"Actually, yes," Corcoran said. It was at that moment that he realized how he could help save the life of Castelleno. *I'm going to serve him with an order to testify at the hearing.*

"All right, then, I'll issue the order. Get me a list of those who will be testifying, and I'll see to it they are so notified."

Walking back to the sheriff's office, Bellows questioned Corcoran. "You have an interesting look on your face, Corcoran. What are you planning?"

"Castelleno, as one of Gordon Hatfield's partners, will have to testify at the insurance hearing, Art. We can keep Phelps in town and possibly keep Rosita from killing Castelleno if they are both served with the stay-in-town order."

Ed Connor and Lou Foster were in the office, drying

out, when Corcoran and Bellows returned. "Got the order from Trimble," Corcoran said. "Need one more name on the witness list, sheriff. Hatfield's third partner, Alphonso Castelleno."

"Of course," Connor said. "It's gonna be a short hearing, though. Anderson's dead, Wellington's dead, and neither Phelps nor Castelleno owned the property when it burned down." Connor took a quick glance at Bellows. "How does all this work as far as the insurance company is concerned?"

"Probably a moot question, sheriff, since the fire was caused by arson. I've sent all the information off to San Francisco and will wait for their reply before trying to answer your question. The insurance was in the name of the business known as the Eureka House Hotel and Saloon and only included the names of Hatfield and Phelps. Castelleno wasn't mentioned and neither was the fact that the outstanding loan was overdue and in jeopardy of being foreclosed on. In my opinion, Wellington was up to his neck in this conspiracy."

"Looks like your company is going to be sending a team of attorneys this-a-way," Corcoran said. "In the meantime, I have a murder that hasn't been solved, we have a possible murder being planned, and I hope Mr. Noah is building an ark somewhere close to us."

That broke up the meeting. The sheriff stayed at his desk, making out the list of witnesses for the hearing. There was a beautiful little tin flask at his side, and the others planned to make their way to the warmth and entertainment at the Bonanza Club.

"I'll get this up to the courthouse a little later. Try to

keep track of Phelps. Lou, more than likely Trimble will ask that a deputy pass out these travel restrictions. That would be you."

Foster had more than enough strength to let out a massive groan as he walked out the door.

CHAPTER TWENTY-FIVE

"Looks like this storm has about blown itself out," Corcoran said. "No sun yet but the wind's sure died down. You fellers go on to the Bonanza, I'm going to have a talk with Abe Afeldt." Corcoran turned up toward the livery and watched Foster and Bellows fight their way across the muddy main street.

"Howdy, Abe. You building an ark?"

"Might be a good idea, Corcoran. Nope," the blacksmith said. "This here's that wagon I promised before the storm. Must be important to get you out in this mess."

"Afraid it is," Corcoran said. "Heard tell that Bill Phelps was in looking to pick up a wagon and horse. What happened to that fine rig he had?"

"Some hoot-and-holler story that no one could believe, Terrence. Man has tall tales to tell every time he shows up around here. I sold him an old stock horse, but I don't have a single buggy, carriage, or wagon on the place. He said he'd try to find one in Palisade after the storm lets up." Afeldt laughed. "According to Doc Whidby that would be forty days from now."

"Sure hope he's wrong," Corcoran laughed. "Is Phelps's new horse capable of making the ride to Palisade in this weather?"

Afeldt laughed right out, again. "Ain't many that could, Corcoran. That mud down in the valley has to be well more than hock high."

"Get back to your work, Abe. I'm gonna find a hot stove and full bottle. No wind blowing makes it nice. Now to get rid of the rain." *We gotta keep Mr. Phelps and Mr. Castelleno in town and alive until the hearing. Lou said that Castelleno said he and Rosita were getting married late today. Judge Trimble didn't say anything about it. Surely he couldn't have a wedding at the church, just days after burying his wife. He's gonna be dead before the hearing, I'm afraid.*

———

SHERIFF CONNOR HAD his list of witnesses filled out and walked it up to the courthouse. "Lots of mud, still, Tommy, but at least the wind and rain have given it up. Want one of my deputies to serve these papers?"

"As soon as possible, Ed. What exactly is going on? The fire at the Eureka House was pretty much determined to be arson, wasn't it? Why has this hearing taken on such stature?"

"The fire was definitely caused by arson, Tommy, but ownership of the property is being questioned. Add several deaths of people directly connected to the insurance claim, and we've got us a full-fledged circus. I don't think I should say anything more at this time."

"It sounds like there might not need to be a hearing," the justice of the peace said. "Sounds like charges may come out of the hearing. I won't ask any more, Ed. We'll save it for the hearing." He looked at the list. "Just these four names?"

"That's it," Connor said. "I'll send young Foster up for the papers. Stay dry, old friend."

Connor worked his way down to the Bonanza Club and found Lou Foster with Art Bellows along with a platter of hot biscuits and a bowl of gravy. "My good luck, eh?" He slid into a chair and motioned for Cindy Cook to bring another setup. "Rain's quit, wind's gone away, and we'll have sunshine in the morning, boys. You heard it straight from the sheriff and you know the sheriff don't lie."

"Sheriff don't lie, Ed," Art Bellows said, "But everyone else we've come in contact with does. I spent more than an hour going over those papers that Corcoran found on Wellington. Did you read past those first few pages?"

"No," Connor said. "Hell, they pretty much spelled it out for me. Phelps pulled a fast one on Hatfield by getting Castelleno in for a full one-third. I still don't understand why Hatfield never told Phelps or Castelleno that the bank had foreclosed, that they no longer owned anything."

"Wellington found those papers on Anderson's desk when he broke into the bank that night. He was in a deal with Hatfield to burn the building down, get the claim money, and leave the territory. He planned to fight you on the arson charges and force the company to pay the claim. Those foreclosure papers changed everything."

"You said you found something else?" Connor asked.

"Did indeed, sheriff." Bellows sat back in his chair and smiled. "Did indeed. I think I know who killed Maria Castelleno."

Before Bellows could go on, Corcoran came in and joined them. "Looks like someone has contacts in the kitchen. Biscuits and gravy? The gods of ancient Greece didn't eat this good." He caught Cindy Cook as she flew into his lap and had his arms wrapped around tight.

"Got another whole basket of biscuits and another bowl of gravy on its way, big boy. Imagine the heaven if you were married to me, Terrence Corcoran." She jumped from his lap and scurried into the kitchen. Corcoran sat still, a little boy's grin splashed across his rugged face.

"Did I miss anything?"

"Mr. Bellows was about to tell us who murdered Maria Castelleno," Ed Connor said.

"Well, I need to hear that. Go on, sir," Corcoran said.

"Even though he was having relations with the woman, I'm reasonably sure it was Gordon Hatfield who slammed that rock into her head. I think he was getting even, in his way, with Phelps for bringing Castelleno into the partnership, and the old man by way of a lost wife."

"I've had that thought but can't find any credence for it, Art. Have you anything to back that up?" Corcoran asked. "It's more than logical but Hatfield's own words put him out at that barn at the time of the murder. Five miles from the scene. The fastest horse can't make up that kind of time and distance."

"I believe that Hatfield was going to torch the Eureka House, rob the bank by blowing it up, which would destroy those papers, and kill his two remaining partners. He had to kill Maria because she knew too much."

"Certainly does fit, Corcoran," Sheriff Connor said. "No one left to argue the case." He sat still for a moment. "You buy into that, Corcoran?"

"It's more than logical, but as I said, every time I run that scenario I realize I don't have a shred of evidence. Logic ain't courtroom evidence, damn it." He got to his feet and walked around the table and sat back down. "I got a lot of reasons to believe Hatfield murdered Maria Castelleno, but every judge in Nevada would laugh me right out of their court if I tried the case."

"Let's get back to where we are," Connor said. "Lou, go up to the courthouse and get those papers and start serving them immediately. You will be an officer of the court. Don't take no from anyone. Start with Castelleno, then Phelps, then the other two."

Foster smiled and got into his large coat. "At least the rain's stopped. I'll leave notes at the office on my progress," he said, and walked out.

"I just came down from Afeldt's livery. Phelps bought an old horse but couldn't get a wagon. We need eyes on him, Ed. He's got boxes and bags of gold and a great desire to be out of here. He sent a wire to his wife to not come on tomorrow's train. He's gonna run, sure as hell."

"I've already pressed our jailer into service, Terrence," Connor said. "Old Tom Reilly is already on the job. He doesn't move very fast but he's carrying that old short barreled ten-gauge double, so no one will get away," he laughed.

"Castelleno is an arrogant old fool, Ed," Corcoran said. "I think I'll serve his papers." He got up and followed Foster out the door.

"If it's all right with you, sheriff, I'd like to serve the papers on Bill Phelps," Art Bellows said. Connor nodded with a smile and Bellows followed Corcoran out the door. Connor continued smiling when Cindy Cook showed up with a full platter of biscuits.

"Where'd everyone go?"

"It don't matter none, Cindy. I'm still here and that platter do smell good."

CHAPTER TWENTY-SIX

"The entire Eureka County sheriff's office is here? To serve four warrants?" Justice of the Peace Tommy Trimble was laughing as Foster, Bellows, and Corcoran streamed into his chambers. "The sheriff was here a little earlier and indicated this might be quite a bit more than just an insurance hearing."

"You can bet on it, judge," Corcoran said. "First though is keeping many of those involved alive. I have a quick question for you. When the bank forecloses on a loan does the paperwork have to come through you, that is, through the court?"

"No, Corcoran. It becomes a court matter if the party served with the foreclosure refused to give the property up. Sometimes the foreclosure papers are simply served, sometimes by way of an officer of the court. They are legal papers attested to by the contracted loan."

"Thank you," Corcoran said. "Let me have the papers on Castelleno. Lou, I'll serve these. Bellows, you take

Phelps's papers, and Lou, you're stuck with the other two. If we hurry we might just save a life or two."

"Remember, you have to physically hand these warrants to the individual. Don't give them to a third party." Tommy Trimble wasn't going to let them out without that warning. "The hearing is day after tomorrow so this gives the recipients plenty of time to prepare. Good luck to you," he said, handing out the warrants.

Corcoran walked into the stables and saddled Dude for the quick ride out to Castelleno's mine. "Gonna be muddy, old man, but it won't be our first ride in the mud, eh? You and me been to places other people ain't even heard of yet. And done things other people wouldn't do even if you paid 'em."

Corcoran found himself talking too loud and about things he hadn't thought of in years. "On top of all that, Dude old friend, my damn head hurts." He loosened the hurricane strings and let his hat flop onto his back. "That's better. When we get back to town, I'm gonna look up Mr. Bill Phelps and kick his butt all over that little town."

Corcoran noticed the bay hitched to the carriage and standing in front of the mine office/home as he stepped down from Dude. "Interesting," he murmured and knocked on the heavy oak door.

The young boy answered again and tried to refuse entry to the big deputy. Corcoran eased the boy aside and walked into the living room. Rosita Chavez was sitting on the couch but Alphonso Castelleno, instead of sitting next to her, was spread out on the couch with his head in her lap.

"Oh, Corcoran, thank heavens you're here. I've been so worried. My husband, yes we were married just a couple of hours ago, is so sick. Can you help him? I think it's his heart," she said.

You might be sure it's his heart, I'm more sure it's something you fed him. Corcoran knelt next to the old miner and felt his head. "No fever." He felt for his pulse and found it beating hard, then almost stopping, then beating hard again. "Boy," he said to the youngster. "Can you ride?"

"Oh sí, señor. I ride good."

"Take my horse and ride like the wind for town and bring the doctor back with you. Do you understand?" The boy nodded. He was in his young teens, long and skinny but strong. "Hurry now."

Rosita Chavez stood up quickly. "You stay here with your uncle," Rosita said. "I'll take the carriage to get the doctor."

"No, Rosita. Go, boy. Hurry." Corcoran took Rosita Chavez by the wrist and held her tight. "You're staying right where you are. Castelleno's heart is probably the only reason he's still alive. Stronger than your poison. Couldn't wait a day or two, eh? Had to kill him off right away. Get all that money and flee the country, eh? Not this time, woman."

She struggled hard and Corcoran was surprised at the strength the woman had. He pushed her into one of the cane-back chairs and pulled his handcuffs out, cuffing one hand to an arm of the chair. "Don't be giving me no trouble, woman."

He heard the thundering hooves of Dude taking off at a full run for town and knelt back down next to Castelleno who was now shaking hard, quivering, spitting up blood, but mostly unconscious. "Need you to live, old man. What did you give him, Rosita?"

Instead of answering she stood up and swung around hard, the chair latched to her wrist came flying at Corcoran's already wounded head. He fended the chair off and before Rosita could get set for another swing, got to his feet and punched her full in the face.

To his great surprise, Rosita Chavez did not crumple to the floor crying out like a baby. Instead, she took the punch like a young buckaroo in a saloon brawl and swung that heavy chair one more time. It crashed solidly across Corcoran's back, knocking him across the quivering body of Castelleno. He rolled quickly to the floor in time to catch the chair this time when she whirled it in his direction.

"You little heller," he growled and swung a mighty right uppercut connecting with Rosita's jaw, this time knocking the strong woman to the floor, out for the time being. "Damn ropes are on Dude," he murmured. There was a large, six-post table made of heavy mahogany off near a front window in the room and he dragged Rosita to it, undid the cuffs from the chair and hooked them to a table leg. "Let's see you swing that at me, woman."

He sat down in a chair near the fire, gently rubbing his head where some of the wounds opened up from all the exertion. He pulled a kerchief from his pocket and tried to stem the bleeding. "Don't never remember a woman that strong. She could very well have won that round if that chair had hit my head." His voice was loud and clear and Corcoran chuckled letting his emotions come back down.

He started a search, first in the living room and then in the kitchen to see if he could find whatever Rosita had given Castelleno. He found some papers on the large table where Rosita was chained and read them with a snicker.

Marriage license? Handwritten but signed by the two of them. Don't know what she said to the old man to get him to do this, but it must have been mighty impressive. Handwritten marriage license? Ain't no such thing I've ever heard of.

He moved into the kitchen and found what he was looking for. The bottle was labeled in Spanish but it carried the skull and crossbones emblem—universal in naming the contents as poison. "Must have put it in his marriage celebration drink. I've come across some evil women in my long career wearing a badge, but I think Rosita Chavez is the worst." He was mumbling as he moved back into the living room.

Castelleno was thrashing about on the couch, had vomited considerable blood, and was about to fall onto the floor. Corcoran moved to catch him and get him back, but stretched out he was still trying to thrash about. "He'll be dead before the doc gets here, I'm afraid. And you, woman, will spend what time you have left in a cell. Hope they hang you high."

He took the time to add a couple of logs to the fire and found a bottle of brandy on a shelf near what would probably be the old man's desk. He took the time to sniff it, chuckling to himself. *Don't want to be drinking that poison. How could you simply pour some of that and then watch someone drink it. Damn.*

―――――

IT WAS another long hour before Corcoran heard horses ride up to the house. He found Sheriff Ed

Connor driving the doctor's buggy flanked by Lou Foster and Art Bellows. "Thought you might need a little help, Corcoran. Castelleno still alive?"

"Barely," Corcoran said. He was looking all around. "Where's that kid and my horse?"

"Broke his leg jumping off at my house," Doc Whidby said. "Your horse is fine. So is the boy. My nurse has him all wrapped up. Where's my patient?"

Corcoran led the doc and the others into the living room and Doc Whidby shook his head as he knelt by the old man. "Know what she gave him?"

"It's on the table in the kitchen, Doc," Corcoran said. "Label's in Spanish but it's poison for sure. I'll get it."

"Not important now," Whidby said. "The man's dead." He got up and walked slowly into the kitchen and found the bottle. "Oh, dear," is all he said. "Didn't need to bring me out here, boys. No one could have saved this gentleman. Strychnine. Nasty stuff, Corcoran. Tell me what you know about that boy you sent in. Well educated, I'll bet anyone who's got a dollar."

"Some kind of relative living with the old man is what he told me."

"Well, he might just own one of the richest mines in Eureka," Doc Whidby said. "That is, if Castelleno didn't actually marry this woman. I'd better give her a once over, from the looks of her face."

Corcoran laughed and told them about the hand-written marriage license, misspelled words and all. "You be careful getting near her, Doc. She's strong as an ox and mean as any pit viper you've ever met. I made the mistake of cuffing her to that chair there. Whipped it around like it was split reins."

Whidby chuckled. "You ride in the back of my buggy with the lady then, my fine deputy friend."

"No," Corcoran said. "Mr. Foster, this is your first arrest, so you get those honors. Put those hands of hers behind her back and attach the cuffs. Put her in the back of Doc's buggy and tie her legs together. Then tie her tight to the buggy. Don't even think of being nice since she's a woman. She's a murderer, Mr. Foster. Treat her as such."

Corcoran had to smile, remembering the first time he had to arrest a woman and how she had used all those girlish wiles to get him to ease off. *My head still hurts from the beating she gave me with my own handcuffs. My own personal code still stands, though. Treat every woman as a lady until she indicates she doesn't want to be treated that way. It's saved my life more than once.*

She fought Lou Foster enough that Corcoran had to jump in and help. One kick to the groin was one too many and Foster slammed her with his fist, knocking Rosita Chavez out cold.

"I didn't want to do that but it was that or curl up and lie down," the young deputy said. "How is it she's so strong?" Nobody answered and Foster stood up slowly with a terrible look of pain, seeing the others do what they could to hide smirks and grins. "Not nice to laugh at a man's pain," he said.

The ride back to Eureka was uneventful with the exception of loud cursing in Spanish when Rosita gained consciousness. "Ain't right for a girl as pretty as she is to talk that way," Foster said. "And she's a killer too? Ain't right."

CHAPTER TWENTY-SEVEN

IT WAS dark before they got back to town. "We've got work to do, gentlemen, so let's finish the hard part first. Meeting in the office in one hour. Get that woman patched up and behind bars, help Doc Whidby with anything he needs, and get your reports written. One hour, gentlemen, my office."

Sheriff Ed Connor helped get Rosita Chavez untied and, with the strong arms of Lou Foster, got her in the jail. She was screaming and kicking. Even with ropes hanging off her ankles, she tried to bite Foster, and she spit at the doctor. "Doc, you take care of her in her cell. Lou, you and Corcoran in there with him."

Holding her down took both men, and Whidby looked at her face and her wrists and just shook his head. "She's going to have a black eye again, but everything else is just scrapes. She'll be in good enough shape to visit the judge." She kicked at him, and it was Doc Whidby who smacked her down this time. The three men scrambled to get out of the cell.

"She was afraid of the world when she reported the death of Maria Castelleno, Doc. Now, she's a raging tiger. Which one is the real Rosita Chavez? I'm confused. Never met a woman that strong either." Corcoran stopped for just a second. *I just said raging tiger. Doc Whidby said whoever killed Maria Castelleno was in a rage. Have I just helped myself to an answer?*

Corcoran's head was bleeding again, and Doc Whidby had him seated at the sheriff's desk. "Can't answer that, Terrence," Whidby said. "My guess is she's been planning something for a long time, and it just came to a screeching end. She's been cooking at the Bonanza, but those hands are not the hands of a cook and that strength is not the strength of a cook. There's a lot more to that woman than we know. I hope you're able to get to the bottom of it."

He got Corcoran's scalp closed up again, blood flow was stopped, and Corcoran vowed to not wear his hat for a week, not fight with tigers for a week, and not wrestle any bears for a week. Whidby was laughing some as he left the jail. "Knowing you, you'll do all of those things and before dawn tomorrow," he called back.

Connor sat down behind his desk and looked at the spread of papers scattered about. "Did we get one single warrant distributed?" He asked and noticed for the first time that he was alone. The others were either in the back with Corcoran or out doing something. "Probably not," he murmured.

At the prescribed time Corcoran, Art Bellows, and Lou Foster gathered in the office. A fresh pot of coffee was boiling, and Connor was behind his desk. "Were papers served on Bill Phelps?"

"Yes. A most unhappy man," Bellows said. "He was leaving in the morning for Palisade, and I informed him that he could not leave town before the hearing. He of course knew that, being district attorney. I don't think the man will run."

"We know about Castelleno," Connor said. "I wonder if the boy should be there for the hearing. He's apparently Castelleno's closest relative." Connor shook his head. "Normally we would go to the DA for legal direction. Damn it."

"I found Abe Afeldt with no trouble, sheriff," Lou Foster said, "and served him. Mr. Florencio won't be back until tomorrow morning. He's meat hunting for the butcher shop and the Bonanza restaurant."

"We have three open murder cases, gentlemen. Maria Castelleno, Alphonso Castelleno, and Ed Graves. We have an open arson case, and half a dozen dead people that I need reports on. The banker, Anderson, and the insurance investigator, Wellington, were each killed by the other, so just a report. The others, Willoughby, Oakley, and Hank Sawyer will need reports written up as well."

"You're right, sheriff," Corcoran said. "Ed Graves's death is an open murder. He was shot by someone currently unknown. Mr. Bellows and I have a suspect in mind and she's already in jail."

"You're right," Connor said. "Is there an update on any of the other open cases?"

"Might as well close Castelleno," Corcoran said.

"Graves's murder and the killing of Maria Castelleno are very much open cases. So many of the people who were suspected of Maria's death are dead, it hampers my work." Nobody chuckled.

"Our jailer, Tommy Reilly, will be making rounds to keep an eye on Phelps during the night hours. Anybody have something to offer? It's been one hell of a day." No one said anything and Connor stood up, stretched, and reached for his jacket. "No rain, no wind, and no one has died in the last ten minutes. Let's call it a day, gentlemen. First drink's on Corcoran." He was laughing loud and strong as he led the bunch out the door.

———

CINDY COOK HAD ELK STEAKS, fried potatoes, and apple pie on the menu and Jimmy Henderson had a bottle of fine bourbon on the table when the boys arrived. "Seems like they knew we were coming and what we want," Lou Foster said. "I hope that was a big elk. Can't remember being this hungry."

It was an early out for the group. Corcoran walked Cindy Cook home but even that romp ended early. First light found Corcoran at Justice of the Peace Tommy Trimble's house. "Saw lights on, judge. I know it's early, but I think this is important."

"Well, Terrence, I am an early rising sumbitch but you are pushing some." He said it with a smile. Trimble was a tough hombre in his courtroom but had a good sense of humor. "Come on in, the coffee's boiling. Why so early?"

"When Ed Graves was killed Art Bellows and I found

where the shooter had been and were able to track the shooter to Bill Phelps's property. I'm positive the shooter was not Phelps but I'm also positive that the shooter left boots and the rifle somewhere on Phelps's property. Maybe buried, maybe in the carriage house, maybe in the house itself. I'd like a warrant to conduct a full search of that property."

"Search warrants are for specific items, Corcoran. You're aware of that." Corcoran nodded. "What specifically will you be looking for?" He walked to his heavy rolltop desk to write out the warrant.

"The boots and the rifle, judge." He would make sure the gold was still in the area, but it wasn't connected to Graves's murder. "Are you aware that Alphonso Castelleno was killed yesterday? Poisoned by Rosita Chavez. She's in custody now."

"I'm sure the paperwork is on my desk. He was an interesting man. What led to his murder? Well, never mind, it will all come out and I'd rather it be in the courtroom." He finished his writing and folded the warrant. "Do you think the old man killed his wife?"

"No, I'm sure he didn't. I've got her death and Ed Graves's death open at this time along with all the other stuff dealing with the arson at the Eureka House. Thank you," Corcoran said and slipped the paper in his pocket.

He made his way to the Bonanza Club for breakfast with Art Bellows. "Got the search warrant for Bill Phelps's place. Find that rifle and boots and Rosita will hang twice. I've never in my life run into a woman as strong as she is."

"I was talking with a couple of the men who work for

Castelleno, and they said she is an accomplished blacksmith, sharpens many of their rock drills, mends iron
works, even builds iron and steel projects for the mine."
Art Bellows was shaking his head and continued. "She
was not Castelleno's housekeeper."

"Well, just damn me," Corcoran said. "That old man
didn't know how to tell the truth, did he, any more than
she does. This casts some shadows one way and light
another dealing with Maria Castelleno's murder. Did
Rosita have relations with Castelleno before their sham
marriage, all the while being upset with Maria having
relations with several men in town?"

"Let's work on one murder at a time," Bellows said.

"Might be working on just one murderer, Art."
Corcoran smiled, Bellows frowned, and Cindy Cook
brought a platter full of pancakes and said another platter
of elk sausage would be coming out shortly.

———

PHELPS ANSWERED Corcoran's heavy rap on the door
right away. "What is it this time?"

Corcoran handed him the search warrant and stepped
around him into the living room. Bellows waited until
Phelps looked at the paper and followed him in, closing
the door tightly. "I don't understand, Corcoran. Looking
for a rifle and boots? I have several rifles and several pairs
of boots."

"For your sake, I hope we don't find these particular
ones," Art Bellows said. "While we're on the subject,
what was Rosita digging for the other morning?"

"I don't know what you're talking about."

"Oh, yes you do," Corcoran said. He pushed Phelps into a chair near the fireplace and stood over him. "It was the morning you swung something big and heavy at my head and caused this." He took his hat off and Phelps couldn't help seeing the bloody bandages. "You did this that morning. What was Rosita burying or digging up?"

"Wasn't me, Corcoran. I didn't do that."

Bellows stepped in before Corcoran took the district attorney apart, one little finger at a time. "You've been served, Phelps. Don't get in our way and don't leave the house." He turned to Corcoran. "Let's start in the upstairs bedrooms, shall we? Phelps, remember, do not leave this house."

Corcoran wanted to smash Phelps's head into mush but knew that would not help his situation. "By the way, Rosita's in jail, Phelps. Open murder." He waited just long enough to hear the gasp and see Phelps's jaw drop. He smiled and followed Bellows upstairs.

"That brought on a strong reaction. I'd still bet she was burying that rifle and those boots the other morning," Corcoran said. "I don't think what she was doing had anything to do with the gold. I'll bet you all the money in the world that Ed Graves knew about the foreclosure on the Eureka House and Phelps had him killed to keep it quiet."

"I think you're about half right, Corcoran. I'll bet you that Wellington is somehow involved. Remember that I found Phelps and Wellington together in the hotel room."

"Sure, just add another problem to all this," Corcoran

chuckled. They found three rooms upstairs. One was a storeroom filled with boxes, mostly books and files from Phelps's work as an attorney before being elected to his current position. One was a guest bedroom, and the other, Phelps's.

"Is there someone we don't know about?" Corcoran asked.

"I think there was. I think Wellington is the missing link. He seemed to know things that no one else knew, including Phelps. He was running a shake-down operation. I still think that Phelps was behind the murder of Graves. Wasn't the shooter, we know that, but was responsible."

The bedroom searches were quick, but the storeroom search took several hours. "Nothing," Bellows said. "He told you he had several rifles and several pairs of boots. Not up here. Only boots I've seen were more fancy than I'd wear."

They moved downstairs and found Phelps still sitting in the chair Corcoran shoved him into. "Find your boots, gentlemen?"

It was Corcoran who held Bellows back this time. "Not worth the effort, Art." They took the living room apart, the kitchen, and the dining room before heading out to the carriage house.

"Know what we haven't seen?" Corcoran asked. "Not one box or bag of gold coins, my friend. Not one."

"I've got a silver dollar says they're in the carriage house. I'll bet another one that he and Rosita had dug them up and he was cleaning up the bags and boxes when you interrupted the digging and I saw part of the cleaning."

Inside the now-empty barn they did not find the stash of gold, and there were no rifles and no boots. "We followed those muddy boot prints right up to this yard, Corcoran. Did they dig up the gold and bury the rifle and boots? Where is all that gold I saw?"

"The man said he had several rifles, Art. We haven't seen them either. There's a room somewhere in that house we don't know about, hidden behind a wall maybe."

"Or under the house? I haven't seen any indication of a regular cellar. He'd want an easy in and out to move that gold or to hide a murder weapon."

Back in the house they found Phelps still sitting in his chair. "You said you had several rifles, Mr. Phelps. We haven't seen any. Same with boots." Art Bellows walked around behind the chair and simply racked it back and let it fall. "Where would we find those rifles?"

Phelps was a big man, as was Bellows and Corcoran, and it took Phelps a moment to get back on his feet, eyes shining with fury. He lunged at Bellows who, with his two arms locked, caught Phelps just under his neck and whipped those arms straight up. This straightened Phelps up and Bellows punched him hard in the nose.

Phelps took the punch and was about to throw one of his own when Corcoran grabbed him by the shoulder and spun him around, driving a fist hard into the man's groin. Phelps bent double, cried out in pain and Corcoran stood him up and drove an uppercut into Phelps's jaw.

Phelps fell to the floor in agony, doubled over and crying out. "I couldn't hear you," Art Bellows said, bent over, yelling in Phelps's ear. "Where would we find those rifles of yours?"

Phelps wasn't able to answer, and the two men left him to lie on the carpet and went back out to the carriage house. Corcoran made one final, almost cursory look-see around the now-empty barn. "I think I know where they are," Corcoran said. "It just came to me. Let's go. The rifle we're looking for and the boots, too, more than likely are stored with bags and boxes of gold about five miles or so, that way," and he pointed west. "Never thought to take a look in that carriage that Rosita took from here. She didn't run away from him, Art. They're partners. That's why Phelps had that horrified look on his face when I said Rosita was in jail. That rifle and all that gold are in that carriage."

CHAPTER TWENTY-EIGHT

CORCORAN AND BELLOWS agreed not to say anything to Phelps. They simply walked out of the carriage house and made their way back to the courthouse stables and saddled up. "Think he'll try to run?" Bellows asked.

"He's got nothing to run with," Corcoran laughed. It was a quick five-mile jaunt in fresh spring air. The sky was cloudless, but the mud remained and would be around for some time. "I'm sure she's hidden the gold and rifle somewhere in Castelleno's barn or workshop. The horse and carriage were tied up just outside the home."

"Doesn't look like it to me," Bellows said. As they rode into Castelleno's place Corcoran saw the horse and wagon had been moved.

"I hope we're not dealing with somebody else wanting to bash my old head in," Corcoran said. They tied off and walked to the front door, which was opened by the young boy, now in a cast and using crutches. "Hello, Pedro. How you feeling?"

"Está bien, señor. It hurts a little, though. Doctor Whidby brought me home last night. I have something to tell you. Would you like some coffee?"

"Thank you," Corcoran said. "Who moved the horse and carriage?"

"That's what I want to tell you," the boy said. He led them into the living room where a hot fire was burning and left to get the coffee. A full pot and three cups were brought out and he sat down with the men.

"I brought the horse and buggy into the barn, unhitched that beautiful bay to get him fed and watered. He'd been standing out there for hours. Not good for the horse. Not good. When I went to move the carriage, it was so heavy that I had to look inside. I found more gold than I've ever seen in my life, señor. Hundreds of pounds of gold."

Corcoran looked at Bellows and smiled. "Good coffee, son. Was there a rifle along with that gold?"

"I don't know. I shut the door and left right away. I was going to try to ride into town later to tell the sheriff."

"Do you feel well enough to answer a few questions?" Bellows asked. "They might be a little personal but are important, having to do with your uncle's death."

"Tío Alphonso. So sad a way to die. If your questions are about that woman, I'll be glad to answer. She was never nice to anyone."

"How's that?" Corcoran asked.

"She helped Mrs. Castelleno cheat on my uncle and then tried to be close with him. She told lies about me, told lies about mi tía. Tried to get me sent away. She tried to make me drink something but was interrupted when you showed up last night." Pedro's eyes were bright. Was it fear or excitement from the night before?

"That was good timing," Bellows said. "You are one lucky boy. She probably had what killed your uncle in that drink."

"I poured it in the vase there when you came riding up."

"I know you can ride, can you drive a horse too?" Corcoran asked and got a quick affirmative. "Good. Let's check that carriage, get the horse harnessed, and get you back to town. We can talk on the way back."

They spent more than an hour searching the carriage and the barn but could not come up with a rifle. "It's buried or dumped somewhere," Bellows said. "Where are we going to stash all this gold? Pedro's right, there are hundreds of pounds here."

"Sheriff has a large vault just for such things. It'll be safe," Corcoran said. He turned to Pedro. "Do you have any sisters or brothers?"

"No, it's just me. My mother and father were killed two years ago, and I was sent to live with my uncle."

"I'm sure you will become the proud owner of all the Castelleno properties. Someone will have to be appointed your guardian until you reach adulthood, but it'll all be yours. That's why Rosita wanted to poison you along with your uncle. Then, she believed, she would come into ownership."

Corcoran chuckled just a bit before he continued. "Who was it that performed the marriage ceremony? Were you there?"

"Sí, I was there. The mine foreman, Gustavo, he read

something that Rosita gave him. After he left is when she made the wedding drinks for everyone. Mine smelled terrible and I threw it in the plants but tío Alphonso drank his."

"Quite a plot, eh, Corcoran?" Bellows said. "She would have had the Phelps gold and the Castelleno property with few questions asked."

"I wonder," Corcoran murmured. They left Pedro with the doctor and brought the horse and carriage to the courthouse stables after emptying it of all the gold at the office. *This beautiful metal is the source of many dreams, can bring so much joy and pleasure, and can lead to death and destruction as well.*

———

"THAT'S THE WHOLE STORY, SHERIFF," Corcoran said. "Pedro's got a quick mind and told us a great deal about life at the Castelleno manor. Rosita Chavez did have relations with the old man, regularly. She helped Maria set up her meetings with various men here in town and then made her moves on Castelleno."

"How does Phelps fit into all this?" Sheriff Ed Connor poured coffee and sat back in his chair, looking first at Corcoran and then Bellows. "She had his horse and carriage and all his gold. It must have been planned."

"That's my next chore, sheriff. I'm sure it was planned but I need a lot more details. My instincts tell me to arrest Phelps right now for conspiracy to murder Castelleno but it's just a thought. Can't prove a word of it."

"The insurance hearing is tomorrow and after that,

Phelps will be able to leave town. Won't be able to stop him." Connor had a sour look on his face. "What's your plan?"

"Find that rifle, hopefully find those boots. Then hope we can tie them to Phelps. Both Bellows and I are sure that Rosita Chavez shot Ed Graves with Phelps's rifle, wearing his oversized boots to run in and lead us to that hedgerow. Tie them together and we can hold Phelps." The look on Corcoran's face was as sour as the one on Connor's.

"That's a long if, my friend," Connor said. "Lou Foster is serving George Florencio and when he comes back, I'll have him join you at Phelps's place. I don't have to tell you to be careful, Terrence, but you might want to remember that Phelps already smashed your head with something big and hard, and he is a suspect in a couple or more murders." He laughed and reached for that flask one more time.

———

WITH A PICK and shovel they found in the empty carriage house, Corcoran and Bellows had a good-sized hole opened in the soft and muddy ground near the hedgerow. "Ground had been dug deep by Rosita and Phelps," Bellows said. "Did Phelps have the gold in this hole?"

"I'm sure of it," Corcoran said. "Can't imagine digging a hole this big and this deep to hide a rifle." They ran out of freshly dug soil and came up empty. "My guess is that rifle is somewhere out along the valley floor, lost forever."

Lou Foster arrived as they were walking the tools back to the barn. "Good timing, Lou," Corcoran joshed. "As you can see we came up empty. Where would you hide a rifle and boots?"

"If they weren't in the house and weren't buried, I'd try the barn again. Didn't you say that there might be a hidden room in the house too?" Foster asked. "That's a big old house. There could be hidden closets anywhere."

"The staircase," Bellows said. "A room under the staircase. I can almost see it, Corcoran. It surprised me at the time that there wasn't a door leading under those stairs. I'll bet there is one, but well-disguised."

"Take these tools back in the barn, Lou, and take that building apart. Look under, over, and through every nook and cranny in there and then join us in the house." Corcoran led Bellows to the front door of Phelps's house and banged hard. It took two more serious blows on the heavy door before Bill Phelps answered.

"You again. What now?"

"Coming back for seconds, Mr. Phelps," Corcoran joshed. "Need to see a couple more things. You told us you had rifles but we never saw any. Where do you keep them?" Corcoran let his eye wander all over the ground level of Phelps's home, in particular the staircase. Sure enough, there had to be a room under that staircase.

"I have them right over here," Phelps said. He walked to a small closet just off the entryway and reached for the door knob.

"I'll get that," Bellows said, stepping in front of the district attorney. He opened the door and found a rifle rack with three long guns. There were also belts with ammunition, filled holsters hanging on hooks, and boxes of ammunition. "Nice, sir. Do you hunt much?"

"I used to hunt often," Phelps said. "Don't have that kind of energy these days." He wandered back and sat down in the old and worn chair. Corcoran watched the moves and was sure he saw a beaten man, one who simply gave up the fight.

He knows it's over. Knows it's just a matter of time before his whole world collapses. He sent a wire telling his wife not to return, had the gold dug up, and was planning to run and Rosita Chavez interrupted the plans. Corcoran couldn't keep his mind quiet. *Or is this all just one plot? Was he planning to hook up with Rosita and the two of them take over Castelleno's properties?*

Bellows had the three rifles out and was going over them carefully. He looked at Corcoran and shook his head, putting them back in their rack. "Haven't been taken care of for a long time, Terrence. They haven't been dusted, cleaned, or shot for a long time." He walked over to the hallway that led around the staircase and back toward the kitchen and dining room.

He knocked on the wall under the staircase and both he and Corcoran smiled. "Hollow," is all Bellows said. "How do we get in there, Phelps?"

"There's nothing there. There is no door," he answered.

"I'm not sure you really want us to make our own door, sir," Corcoran snapped back. "We will if you insist, though. How do we get in there?"

Phelps sighed, started to get up but sank back into

the depths of the big chair. "I'm sure you can figure it out."

Corcoran looked at the big man and almost felt sorry for him. He was looking at total defeat and failure. Giving up. He saw the man looking across the room to the open closet. *Oh, no you don't.* Corcoran walked over, shut the door, and pulled a heavy table over to block it.

He saw the despair in Phelps's eyes, heard it in his voice, and could almost see the man bolt for one of the revolvers hanging in the closet. *He was going to make a play for one of the pistols in there. Might be an attorney but like most criminals—really dumb.*

Bellows was looking at the wood framing the staircase closet and pushed a time or two at various joints. The one on the lowest side, that is, the staircase side, gave in some and when he released the pressure, a door came open. "Took a real artist to build this," Bellows said. "Spring-loaded and all. Bring a lamp, Terrence, I think we've struck our bonanza."

The closet was small, angled because of the staircase, but standing up against the high wall was a rifle and on the floor next to it, a pair of once-muddy boots. Bellows pulled the rifle out and gave it a close going over. "Unlike his hunting rifles, this one has been recently cleaned, oiled and put away properly, Terrence."

"That's a damn shame," Corcoran said. "We know it's been recently fired and that's all we know. Let's see if we can match that mud with what we found near the Graves shooting?"

Bellows walked off into the kitchen, opened the door, hollered for Lou Foster, and returned. "We can't walk off and leave this," he muttered. Foster came in and Bellows handed him the boots. "Run up to where we thought the shooter was and see if you can come up with a match."

"Whatever you come up with, Lou, will be courtroom evidence. Be as careful with it as you would be with an egg. Got it?" Corcoran said. He walked over to where Phelps was sitting and ripped a slipper off the man, measured it against one of the boots, and smiled. Good fit, sir," he said, handing the slipper back. "Be quick about this but thorough, Mr. Foster. You'll be describing in court what you find. We'll meet you back at the sheriff's office."

"It's scary knowing that," Foster said. He had the boots and walked out. Corcoran smiled trying to remember what it was like in his first few days of being a lawman and just shook his head knowing it was a long time ago.

"Well, now, Mr. Phelps, it looks like it's time for us to have a little chat." Corcoran moved a chair right up close to Phelps's, motioned for Bellows to bring the rifle and join him.

"Can't deny this is your rifle, Phelps," Bellows said. "Monogrammed and all—*WP*—and in silver yet. Why did you kill Ed Graves?"

"That's not my rifle. Never seen it before."

Corcoran looked at the rifle. "It's fitted out for .45-70, Phelps. All your other rifles are standard 45 caliber." He got up and walked to the closet with the other rifles, picked up a box and returned. "Yup, an open box of .45-70. Not yours either, Mr. Phelps?"

"Never seen 'em before."

"And him being an attorney." Art Bellows scoffed, got up, and walked to stand near the fire. "It's my firm belief that you stood in that muddy yard and shot Ed Graves dead and ran back here, dumped the boots, and hid the rifle and boots. What do you think, Corcoran?"

"Certainly fits with everything we know about Graves's death. That's the murder weapon, those are the boots, and you, sir, are the murderer. Want to talk about it some? For instance, why did you want Ed Graves dead? He was your partner's attorney."

Bill Phelps sat rigid in his chair, he wouldn't look at either man, he just stared into the fire. "We know that Ed Graves found out about the bank foreclosing on the Eureka House property, Mr. Phelps," Corcoran continued. "Is that why he had to die? Did Hatfield know? How is it you knew? Mr. Anderson probably served the foreclosure notice on Graves because he was Hatfield's attorney. Did he also serve you? Or did that sleazy Richard Wellington tell you. What about Castelleno?"

Phelps never moved. He blinked his eyes a time or two, licked his dry lips, and stared into the fire. "Come now, Mr. District Attorney," Art Bellows said, "you must have something to say in the matter. There's a lot at stake here. Did you help Hatfield burn the property down? Or are you the one who shot Hatfield from ambush?"

Phelps never moved. Stoic was how Corcoran would write it down in his report.

"Let's change the subject, then, shall we?" Corcoran said. "Let's talk about Rosita Chavez for a minute." For the first time, Phelps started to turn his head toward the two investigators, caught himself, and turned back to the fire. "She had all your gold when she killed your other partner, Castelleno. I hope she was good in bed because she wasn't very good handling your wealth."

Bellows laughed right out at the comment and Corcoran saw Phelps stiffen up like an iron rod. "How did you let her get away with all that gold anyway? You're at least twice her size." Corcoran snickered but couldn't help remember just how strong the lady was. "Did she beat you up and take it? Or did she sweet talk you into letting her have it?"

Bellows picked up on where Corcoran was leading the man. "Maybe you and Rosita were going to be together at the Castelleno Mine, eh? Maybe after she killed the old man and the mine property became hers, you two would get together and share the wealth. Is that why you told your wife not to return?"

Phelps jumped to his feet and stormed toward Bellows. Corcoran stood up fast and intercepted the man with a stunning punch to the side of his head, sending Phelps flying across the room. Bellows walked over, jerked him to his feet, and dragged him back to his chair. "Sit," he said. "I think we have some of our questions answered," Bellows said. "He's all yours, Corcoran."

Corcoran jerked Phelps to his feet. "It gives me great pleasure to say this, Mr. Phelps. You're under arrest for the murder of Ed Graves." He spun the heavy man around and put the handcuffs on him. "Let's go to jail, shall we? Make sure the doors are locked, Mr. Bellows, we don't want to lose any of this evidence."

It was a sight enjoyed by many in the little mining town of Eureka that fine spring day, watching Terrence

Corcoran and Art Bellows march Bill Phelps through town in his slippers and dressing gown. There were a few catcalls but more stunned faces and open mouths, wide eyes, and gasps. Corcoran handed Phelps over to the jailer, Tommy Reilly, and plopped down in the sheriff's chair.

"I don't think he's the one," Bellows said.

"I don't either. I'm still under the impression that Rosita killed Graves but I think another little grilling will get him to tell us. He is part of the conspiracy, though, and that'll get him locked up for some time."

Tommy Reilly came back out in a hurry. "They're yelling at each other, Terrence. Some nasty threats being made back there."

Corcoran smiled and walked to the door to listen for a moment before going in. "All right, now. You lovebirds calm it down." He motioned for Reilly to move Phelps to the last cell in the line, reserved for the most rowdy of their guests. Instead of bars it had solid walls and a solid iron door. The only light in the cell came from a high window just twelve inches long by five inches high.

"Mr. Bellows and I will be back to talk some, Phelps. There will be an insurance hearing in the courthouse tomorrow morning. Try to get some rest." Corcoran had a smile on his face as he walked back into the office. "Mr. Reilly, be as careful as possible when you're around Rosita Chavez. She is more dangerous than anyone we've had the pleasure of hosting."

CHAPTER TWENTY-NINE

LOU FOSTER HAD the boot with the dried mud on it and was comparing the traces of mud when he saw the empty brass casing and picked it up. He knew the mud was a match and hoped the empty brass would be as well. It was a quick almost lope back down to the sheriff's office.

"Good work, Lou. Outstanding," Corcoran said. "We have the rifle, an open box of .45-70 rounds found at Phelps's home, and now a match of mud and an empty brass casing. Calibers match, mud matches, boot size matches. Mr. Phelps is going to prison or the gallows."

"Even if he didn't do the crime?" Bellows asked. "I still believe it was Rosita who killed Ed Graves."

"I do too, Art," Corcoran said. "But I also believe that Bill Phelps was as involved as if he had pulled the trigger. We need to get him to implicate her. Then we get her as the shooter and he as the conspirator. Let's let him sit in that lonely chamber back there for a few hours and then go have a talk with him."

"A long talk with Rosita might give us something to talk about," Bellows chuckled.

"Mr. Foster. You and Mr. Reilly take a wagon and go to Phelps's place and bring all those guns and ammunition back up here for safe keeping. I want the dirty guns to remain dirty. Don't try to wipe them clean at all. We'll get 'em labeled and safe."

Corcoran nodded at Bellows, and they walked back into the cell area. "Hello, Rosita. Need to have a chat. How are you feeling? That jaw still hurt some, does it?" Corcoran was lighthearted, almost flippant in his approach, doing what he could to get the already angry woman even more angry.

"Was it your idea to kill Ed Graves? Was it because he knew about the foreclosure? That would end the insurance payoff, right?" Corcoran pulled a bench over near Rosita's cell but well back from the bars. She sat on her cot and glared at him.

"How did you get tangled up in all this, anyway? A friend of Maria Castelleno who had regular, shall we say, meetings with Phelps and now you doing the same? Phelps have something special? It isn't money."

Bellows almost howled he was laughing so hard, and Rosita threw her tin cup hard at Corcoran. "You are a filthy man. Maria was a whore. Deserved to die. Castelleno needed my love but kept saying how much he loved Maria. Bill Phelps is a weakling, not a man at all."

Corcoran stood up and walked into the office, Bellows right behind him. "Did she just say that she killed Maria Castelleno?" Corcoran sat down behind the desk and wrote for a few minutes. "Read this. Do I have it as close as possible?"

"That's what I heard," Bellows said, handing the sheet of paper back. "It was as close to a confession as I've ever heard but I don't think what you've written would stand up in court."

"No, I don't either, but it sure is someplace for us to continue prodding. Maria was having relations with Phelps and Hatfield and the two of them talked about their activities with each other. Rosita was having relations with Castelleno and was angry about Maria's relationships. Whew, Mr. Bellows, I don't want to know more. I don't."

Bellows chuckled and walked around the office. "Rosita says she is offended by Maria's behavior but sleeps with one of the men involved as well as Maria's husband. Misguided morals, Terrence. She was sleeping with Castelleno strictly for his money. So why did she have relations with Phelps? More money? A gold mine wasn't enough?"

The laughter from both men greeted Sheriff Ed Connor's entry. "What brought all this on?"

"Have a seat, sheriff," Corcoran said getting up from Connor's desk. "We have another guest back there. Bill Phelps will be staying with us for a while." He poured everyone cups of coffee and drew up a chair next to the desk. "You're probably not going to like what I'm about to lay out here."

"It's an everyday happening, Terrence. One gets used to it," Connor said. He was wearing about half a smile, though. "Before you give me your problems, let me give you one. What are we going to do about Rosita Chavez? We are not set up to have female prisoners, Terrence, and now with Phelps in there, we simply can't have them in our jail at the same time."

"We surely can't let one go," Corcoran said. He saw the set to the sheriff's jaw and knew the problem just became his. "All right, Ed, I'll come up with an answer. Now it's my turn."

Corcoran spent half an hour bringing Sheriff Connor up to date and the three men walked down to the Bonanza Club for cold beer and more talk. "I don't think what Chavez said could be interpreted as a confession, Corcoran. More likely just an indication of how she felt, how she was almost glad the way things turned out. However, the evidence around Graves's death is good. Very strong."

Connor and the other two were at a table near the front windows of the Bonanza, a bottle of bourbon in the middle of the table and flagons of beer in front of each man. "Why do you think it was not Phelps who did the actual shooting even though you've tied all the evidence around the man's neck?"

"Both Bellows and I followed the muddy trail from the scene to Phelps's yard," Corcoran said. "We both commented on the clumsy trail, that the person running was having trouble with the boots. We're sure someone was wearing outsized boots. We thought right from the first, that it was Rosita wearing Phelps's boots."

"You think she was implicating him?" Connor sat back letting the thought sink in. "Knowing she skipped with his gold that thought makes sense." He sighed and took a long drink of cold beer. "You've got enough evidence to send Phelps to Carson City for a long time. Are you sure you want to pursue this?"

"I'm afraid so," Corcoran said. He was quiet, thinking. *It would be easy to just let Phelps hang for Graves's murder. The evidence is strong as hell but that's not my style. She acted on his behalf, or she purposely implicated him. Either way, she's going to hang. Connor is right, though. How do we prove any of it?*

"I'm going to have a long talk with Bill Phelps," Corcoran said. "I'm going to lay this out in bold letters. His response should give me the answers we're looking for."

———

CORCORAN LEFT his gun in the office and made his way to the solitary confinement cell and Bill Phelps. "I want you to listen to me hard, Mr. Phelps," he said. "Your rifle was used to kill Ed Graves. I followed muddy prints from the murder scene to your yard and your boots match your feet and the mud matches the scene. We even have the empty shell that was ejected following the killing."

Corcoran sat back on the cot watching Phelps's face as he laid out the crime. Phelps had an intent look on his face, actually made facial movements twice, and sucked in his breath once during the commentary. "You're the district attorney, sir. If I brought you this kind of evidence, what would your reaction be? How would you respond, sir?"

Phelps had a helpless look on his haggard face,

shrugged his shoulders, and slowly let his breath out. Irony was not a part of his makeup but the slightest smile that came across his face showed it in every way. "I'm afraid I'd ask for the death penalty, Corcoran, but I didn't do what you just lined out. It wasn't me."

Corcoran could see him squirm, as uncomfortable a man as he had seen in a long time. "I'm sure you are aware of who it was, Mr. Phelps." He stood up and walked to the small chair Phelps was scrunched into. "Who shot Ed Graves?"

"I don't know." Anger flushed his face and Corcoran saw his fingers double into a fist, then release. "It wasn't me, Corcoran. I didn't do it."

Corcoran bent down over the man and said, in a strong voice, "Who set you up to die, Mr. Phelps?" Phelps cringed and ducked his head but didn't say anything. "Would it be the same person who stole all your gold? Or did she shoot Ed Graves because the two of you were working together?"

"No," he murmured. "No." He slowly lifted his head and Corcoran saw questions in his face. His eyes were pleading for Corcoran to stop, to leave him alone, to quit the tormenting. "She wouldn't do that," he said in such a low and quiet voice that Corcoran wasn't sure he heard it. "Not Rosita. She wouldn't do that."

"She wouldn't, Mr. Phelps? Come now, sir. She's in a cell less than twenty feet from where we are because she killed Alphonso Castelleno." Corcoran paced around the small cell stopping in front of Phelps.

"Did she kill Ed Graves?" The question was direct and strong, and Phelps shrunk back from it.

"Yes," he murmured and tried to make himself even smaller. His head was bent so that his chin was all but driven into his chest, his arms were wrapped tightly about himself, and he even drew his feet up.

Corcoran had him, knew it but knew this wasn't the time to back off. Now was the time to drive spikes through the man's heart, to slam him across the side of the head with a mace, to draw blood by the gallon.

"What was the plan, Phelps? For the two of you to kill Castelleno after Rosita's sham marriage to the man? For the two of you to own the Castelleno property?"

"No!" Phelps screamed it out. He jumped to his feet, his fists doubled, glaring at Corcoran. The big deputy slugged Phelps in the jaw with a mighty right cross sending the man hard into the steel wall. He crumpled to the floor, wrapping into a fetal position.

Corcoran set the chair back up and grabbed Phelps by the back of his shirt, jerked him to his feet, and forced him into the seat. "Make a stupid move like that again and you'll be having a long talk with Doctor Whidby, Mr. Phelps. If what I said wasn't the plan, then what was it? Surely a man of your background would have a plan."

"There was no plan. We were not working together. She found out about the gold I had, found out about the foreclosure, and knew I would not be getting the fire insurance payout." Once Phelps got started, he couldn't stop talking. Corcoran sat back on the cot and just let him go.

"I knew about Hatfield's plan to torch the Eureka House but wasn't aware of any of the other things he had planned. Unfortunately, Rosita Chavez also knew. The three of us discussed it two days before Maria Castelleno was killed. Hatfield had plans to kill off Castelleno and sweet talk Maria into marrying him. All of this was discussed."

"Rosita knew all of this?" Corcoran asked and Phelps nodded. *This must have been when she decided it was she who was to marry into Castelleno's fortune, not Hatfield. Did she kill Maria too? I've got to get with the sheriff and Art Bellows right away.*

"We're not through, Mr. Phelps. You're sure it was Hatfield who was making plans for he and Maria, not you? You're sure, sir?"

"My only plans were to get the insurance money in a large trunk with my gold and move to San Francisco. The bank's foreclosure would change all that. Ed Graves told Hatfield and Rosita accidentally found out about my gold and the foreclosure. That's all there was to it. I had nothing to do with Graves's death."

"Thank you," is all Corcoran said and walked out of the crimped cell.

CHAPTER THIRTY

"HOW MANY PEOPLE were after Castelleno's mine and fortune, Corcoran?" Ed Connor was at his desk wagging his shaggy head back and forth. "Hatfield? Looking to kill the old man. Chavez? Looking to do the same. And the stupid district attorney? Only looking for a good bedmate in Chavez." Sheriff Connor was having some fun and gasped. "Almost makes me sick to my stomach thinking about it. Almost," he laughed.

The office filled with gentle laughter. "And the end result took place on a lovely day for a picnic." Connor was rocking in his old chair. He had some fun but at the same time, was both angry and sad. "I hope you can convince Judge Trimble that we probably don't need an insurance hearing. We need a multiple murder hearing."

Corcoran walked out and up the hill toward the courthouse. *Rosita, hearing Hatfield say how he planned to kill off Castelleno and marry Maria must have triggered her plans. She was already having an affair with the old man so how best to get rid of Maria?* Corcoran shook his head. "No," he murmured. "No. The question should be how best for me to prove that Rosita killed Maria."

He still had his doubts, was still of the opinion that it was a spurned wishful lover who killed the woman. The killing was so vicious and so mean in the way it was handled. "A heavy rock slammed over and over into the woman's face shows a level of hatred I don't think I've ever known or seen," he murmured. "At the same time, I know she has the strength to carry it off. Am I the only one with doubts about her guilt?"

Justice of the Peace Tommy Trimble was in his office staring up at the ceiling, about half asleep, when Corcoran knocked and walked in. "Terrence Corcoran, come in. I was just thinking about the hearing."

"That's why I'm here, but I have a wagon full of problems that I need your help with." He laid out the entire situation and Trimble sat in amazed silence through the program. "The best I can say is that we have several major crimes including murder and all related, one to the other. Interestingly, it's the arson that forced the investigation in this direction."

"You have more than the problems you just outlined, Corcoran," Trimble said. "You have a county without a district attorney. This needs to be taken to the district judge, Eric Bayliss, who would in turn appoint a prosecutor. You can arrest all the people you want, Terrence, but it takes a prosecutor to get them into a courtroom. We can't even hold a preliminary hearing without a prosecutor."

"Is it you who goes to the district judge or is it the sheriff? Heaven help us if we have to go to the county commissioners." Corcoran caught himself seeing the frown come across the judge's face. He needed to change the subject.

"I've got a woman at that jail, judge. We don't have facilities for women. We can't have women and men in the same jail and I sure as hell can't ask that one or the other be released on bail."

"You take care of that problem and I'll get Judge Bayliss down here. He's in Elko and I'll send him a wire. I'll have an answer for you in less than a day, I'm sure."

———

"GET IT ALL SQUARED WITH TRIMBLE?" Sheriff Connor asked when Corcoran returned.

"He'll bring in District Judge Bayliss who will have to have a prosecutor assigned to the county. We may have our guests for longer than would be normal."

"Bayliss is a tough old bird, Terrence." Connor smiled and looked up at the ceiling. "He'll sift through all the nonsense and we're likely to have a hanging or two around here."

"As far as Rosita is concerned," Corcoran said, "I'm going to have a talk with Doc Whidby, Jimmy Henderson, and Cindy Cook and see if we can come up with some kind of answer. You are absolutely right, though. She can't stay in our jail."

Corcoran found Jimmy Henderson behind the bar at the Bonanza Club and called for a cold beer. "I need to find a place to hold Rosita Chavez, Jimmy. We don't have any facilities for women at the jail. Only run into this a couple of times in the past. Chavez is as strong as old Abe Afeldt and far more dangerous than any man you can think of. I'm not asking for one of your hotel rooms unless you have one made of steel bars."

"When the county finally agreed with Ed Connor and built your new building with the jail, they planned on converting the old jail in the basement of the courthouse into offices, which have never been built. Those cells are still there."

"Forgot all about that," Corcoran said. "Lou Foster is about as strong as Afeldt, so he should be able to control her." He tried to remember what was in the cellar as he made his way back to the office. *Food was brought in just like we do now, and there was a latrine, somewhat private, not buckets like some places have. Lou Foster and Tommy Reilly would always be there until the trials are over.*

He and Foster made their way down the stone steps into the courthouse basement, carrying lamps. "Ever been down here, Corcoran? From the dust and dirt, I'd say it's been a long time since anyone has."

"The new office and jail were built eight years ago, Lou. This is my first visit. Only heard stories." Corcoran fumbled with the ring of keys he got from the court clerk and got a steel door opened at the bottom of the staircase. "They carved this out of solid bedrock." He looked around as they entered a large room with rock walls and floor. "Probably had assays done on every blast too," he chuckled.

"Would have been interesting if they'd found gold," Foster joshed.

There was an area that probably held a desk and

chairs, a stove still connected to the upstairs chimneys, and two cells. Off to the right of the cells was the privy, which had an exhaust pipe that went up through the ceiling. "Primitive as hell, but somewhat private for a woman, and safe for a killer," Corcoran said.

"Having to let her out of her cell every time she needs to use the facilities will be more than dangerous. Sure can't let old Reilly handle that." Foster frowned and walked over to the cell closest to the latrine. "Need to extend the cell to incorporate the hole."

"Go get Abe Afeldt, Lou, and bring him down here. Get him started on that. Highest priority. Good thinking, Mr. Foster. We'll get a couple of the county people down here to clean it up and to help Abe if he needs it. I want this ready to be occupied by tomorrow morning at the latest."

———

THE CELL WAS EXTENDED in record time and Connor had most of his crew ready to move Rosita Chavez to her new digs. "Stand here with your back to the bars, Chavez," Corcoran said. "Put your hands behind your back and through the bars."

Rosita refused to get off the cot and just sat staring at the floor. "If we have to do it the hard way, we will," Connor said. "Do what Corcoran told you." Rosita didn't even give a hint that she heard the sheriff, and Connor nodded to Corcoran and Foster to enter the cell. The two unarmed men moved in and before they could get the door slammed shut, Rosita sprang at them.

Her powerful arms and shoulders were swinging wildly as she raced for the open door. Art Bellows slammed the cell door shut just as she got there and Corcoran, his nose bleeding from a wild punch, grabbed one arm.

"Get the other one, Lou, and we'll pin her to the bars." Foster used both hands to grab Rosita's other arm and hung on tight as she wrenched, kicked, and spit at the two men. They pushed her back to the bars and Connor came up from the other side and got the hand-cuffs on the wildcat. Connor held on to the chain connecting the cuffs, keeping Rosita pinned to the cell bars.

"Hold her tight, Ed. Get those leg-irons on, Lou," Corcoran snarled through the dripping blood. He was on his knees with both arms around the woman's legs as Lou Foster managed to evade nasty kicks and get leg-irons in place. The chains connecting the irons were short and Rosita was forced to make small steps, not able to kick, and changed her tactics to spitting and screaming.

"Let her get it out of her system," Connor joked as they started to move her from the cell into the outer office. "Gonna be one hell of a show for our fine citizens, getting her up to the courthouse."

Rosita Chavez had her own agenda and simply let herself fall to the floor almost taking Lou Foster with her. She tried to pin Lou Foster down with just her weight, not having the ability to use her arms or hands and he squirmed free. All the tugging and lifting failed to get the woman to her feet. She simply went limp and that was it.

"We can't walk her up that hill, sheriff. Even if she

was cooperating, taking six-inch steps, it would take us an hour or more," Art Bellows said. "Best to put her in the back of a wagon."

"Go get Doc Whidby's little wagon, Lou," the sheriff said. "Might want to bring him back with you. One of us or her is surely gonna need his attention."

Corcoran stood back, wiping more blood from his nose and thought about what he'd just seen. *What was it Doc Whidby had said? Someone in a rage was responsible for Maria's death. I think we just saw that. I'm more than convinced now that Maria was killed by Rosita Chavez.* He laughed a little to himself. *Now I have to prove it.*

———

IT TOOK the combined efforts of the sheriff, his deputies, and an insurance investigator to get Rosita out of the office and into the back of the wagon. "Sit on her, Corcoran. You, too, Foster. Art, you drive. I ain't even getting in the wagon," Ed Connor said. "I'll walk."

A screaming woman near the sheriff's office was sure to bring people out from nearby businesses and homes. When the scene involved three large men wrestling with the screaming woman, the numbers of the curious increased rapidly. "Let's try not to make a horrible scene, gentlemen." Connor knew he faced a courthouse filled with workers as well and had to get Chavez into the building and down into the cellar with as little drama as possible.

"Mr. Afeldt, would you be kind enough to try to keep all the lookers back? Corcoran, you take her feet and,

Bellows, you and Foster take her shoulders. Do your best not to injure the prisoner but on the other hand there's no need to be kind."

Connor was sure it was the longest hour of his life when they finally pulled the cell door closed and locked. "Mr. Reilly, this is the most dangerous prisoner we've ever had locked up. Do not approach those cell bars for any reason. Do not attempt to help her in any way at all. She will do everything she can to entice you close enough to kill you. Never carry the cell keys unless one or more of us is here with you."

"I understand," Tommy Reilly said. The look on his face after watching all the proceedings proved what he said. "Will there be someone here with me?"

"Mr. Foster and you will split the days with her. She'll be alone at night. She'll get two meals a day brought up from the Bonanza Club." Connor wiped his forehead with his sleeve and let out his breath. "Questions?"

"Just one," Corcoran said. "Who's buying the first drink?"

CHAPTER THIRTY-ONE

ERIC BAYLISS, district judge for north central Nevada, was a large man who fully enjoyed his meals, several of which he ate daily. Along with his bulk he was a jolly man who drank more than most men could even wish for, and loved the ladies, none of whom he could satisfy. He had lost that ability a few years ago and replaced those desires with food and booze.

On the bench he was a lion on the prowl. Attorneys were seen with tears on their cheeks after a dressing down, witnesses were called liars right out, and things were often testy if the judge disapproved of an attorney's handling of the case. It was a wise man who played the judge's game.

Bayliss's arrival on the Eureka and Palisade Railroad was almost a circus on a mid-spring morning flush with blue skies and cotton candy clouds. "Someday the government will understand and appreciate the needs of a district judge and provide us with private rail cars, good food, and select brandies. Traveling with the herd is below our dignity." His rolls of fat were in considerable motion following his comment.

"Where's Trimble? You here, Tommy?"

"Right here, judge. I think you know Eureka County Sheriff Ed Connor, and this is his chief deputy, Terrence Corcoran."

"Corcoran? Ha! The man who shot the sheriff in Virginia City. Been looking forward to meeting you, Corcoran. Good job in White Pine County too. Trimble thinks we have a real mess here. What say you, chief deputy?"

"I rarely argue with a judge," Corcoran said.

"A politician, are you?" Bayliss laughed right out. "We'll get along just fine. Where's my carriage? They better have good food at this Bonanza Club, Trimble. I haven't eaten since that slop on the train."

It was a parade up the road and into town. Many townspeople came out of their shops and homes to wave a welcome to Judge Bayliss who responded in kind, as if he were a returning hero. The entourage spread through the saloon and connecting restaurant. Jimmy Henderson was prepared having himself and Tony Soma working behind the bar.

Cindy Cook had a new girl helping in the kitchen and met the judge with a grand smile. "We have sliced roasted elk, leg of lamb, and the finest beef available from the Diamond Valley, judge. What's your pleasure?"

"That sounds just fine," Bayliss said. "Yes, indeed, that sounds just fine."

Cindy stood still, waiting for the judge to say which of the items he preferred before it finally struck her that he wanted full courses of each. "Coming right up," she giggled and ran off for the kitchen. The rest of the group would get along with whatever might be left over.

———

BAYLISS WAS at the courthouse conferring with Justice of the Peace Trimble for most of the rest of the day. Nothing could proceed until the two of them were able to appoint a prosecuting attorney. Nevada had been growing rapidly over the last many years and anytime you're dealing with the frontier, gold, silver, and human beings there will be a need for attorneys.

"Stanley Packett it is, then," Eric Bayliss said late in the afternoon. "Get a wire off to him immediately. He needs to be here in no less than two days."

———

CORCORAN AND BELLOWS sat at a table with flagons of cold beer at hand. Cindy Cook was planted securely on the deputy's lap, nuzzling his neck and ear. "Bayliss is a stickler, Bellows. We have to have our facts in perfect order. I've never met this Packett fellow. He's coming to us from Reno."

"The case against Rosita is the strongest. She flat-out poisoned the gentleman. Are you still planning to hang Ed Graves's murder on Phelps?"

"Have to unless Rosita gets all ghoulish on us and demands otherwise. I really don't think she'll confess, and I'm not sure if Phelps will implicate her. He flat-out told me, but I was alone in there. Not admissible. It's Maria Castelleno's death that still hangs with no one charged. I want to have another one-on-one interview with Rosita Chavez. There's something that tells me she did it, but I still have shadows of doubt."

"Because of the men she teased? Or is it something else?" Bellows asked. "After what you told me about Abe Afeldt's anger, I'd certainly give him a spot on your list."

"He's there but has a tight alibi. Florencio is there but has a tight alibi. Even Castelleno is there with a tight alibi. Even if he was at the mine, Castelleno could very well have hired the killing."

"The Chavez woman is mentally unstable, Terrence," Bellows said. "Even if she confesses, this Judge Bayliss might not accept it. How else would you prove she did it?"

"Right now, Art, I can't. Why don't you join me as I talk with her. Maybe you'll hear something that I miss, or maybe come up with that special question that answers everything about life."

They were still chuckling as they made their way down the stone staircase and into the old jail. "Glad you're here, Lou. I want you to listen as I have a chat with Rosita. Any problems so far?"

"She's spent the last hour crying. Very softly, hard to hear, but crying. I think the reality of her killing Castelleno is hanging heavy. She knows she could hang and is scared."

"Have you talked to her at all? Or just been here."

"At first she wanted me to sit close so we could talk but I knew better than to do that and ignored her. That's when the crying started. I thought it was a ruse, you know, a way to get me close, but it's been going on for some time. Her crying is real."

"We'll see." Corcoran wasn't ready to believe that, particularly after the way she had screamed and fought like a mule whenever anyone tried to get her to do something. He and Bellows moved toward the cell door and handed their gun belts to Foster. "Shoot her dead if she gets the better of us," Corcoran said. "And she could."

Corcoran unlocked the cell and threw the key ring back to Foster. "Lock us in tight and listen to everything we say. The least little thing could be the most important." He sat on a chair across from Rosita who was sitting on the cot, with Bellows standing back and off to the side. Rosita's face was flushed, her eyes red and swollen, and her cheeks damp with tears.

Looks like Mr. Foster knew what he was talking about. She's an angry and mean woman who still has a heart. "Having a hard time facing all of this?" Corcoran asked. He spoke softly, almost as a friend would and she turned her face up to him. Her eyes were pleading but her mouth was set in anger, ready to snarl, bite, or rip at his face.

"Tell me about your relationship with Maria Castelleno. Some have said you were close friends, others say you didn't much like her. What do you say?" Corcoran's voice was soft and friendly and the first thing he noticed was the grimace when Maria's name came up.

Rosita didn't move about or seem concerned with the

exception of her eyes. They were filled with hate. "She was not a good woman. Not a good wife to her man. She was a whore and deserved to die."

"Is that why you killed her, Rosita? Because she was unfaithful to Castelleno. Did you plan to kill her at the picnic or did the opportunity just happen?"

"Mr. Hatfield was supposed to meet her for the rendezvous but sent a boy with a note saying he couldn't make it. It was perfect. She was slumped, holding the note, and I took advantage of the situation. That horrible man made it possible."

"Why do you have a relationship with Mr. Phelps if you think Hatfield was so horrible. Phelps, too, had relations with Maria, regularly."

"Money, Mr. Corcoran. Gold." Rosita sat straight up, squared her shoulders and wiped at her eyes. Corcoran sat back a bit, not sure what the transition would lead to. "I own the Castelleno mines and I have thousands of dollars of Mr. Phelps's money. I am the mistress of the property now." Proud and boastful, Rosita's whole character changed with that simple statement.

"You did everything for the money? Not because Maria was unfaithful and you had to stop that from continuing?"

"What does it mean, unfaithful? She didn't respect her marriage. Neither did that old fool she was married to. Respect for a marriage is the most important thing and neither had it. Now, I have all their property, all their money, all their gold."

Corcoran had many things to say, none of which

would get said. *She talks about respect for marriage while sleeping with the man who is married to the woman who has no respect for marriage. My lord, but she doesn't have the least idea of what she's talking about. And all of this for money.*

Corcoran nodded to Bellows and walked to the cell door as Foster came over to let them out. "She doesn't know, does she?" Bellows asked.

"No, I'm sure she does not realize that young Pedro is the mine's new owner even though she knew enough to try and kill him as well. She's lost her mind and I wonder just how Judge Bayliss will handle this situation. She's living in a fantasy world right now. Actually, she has probably been in that world for a long time considering what we know of her background."

"Her anger at her life turned to desire for what the others had, which turned to greed. Let's get this written up and turned over to the judge. It is possible that Packett might not have to show up. The only thing Phelps is guilty of is conspiring to have Ed Graves killed."

Corcoran chuckled at the comment but stopped suddenly and turned back to Rosita. "Just out of curiosity, Rosita, why did you kill the attorney, Ed Graves?"

Bellows was caught as much off guard as was Chavez and stood next to Corcoran with his mouth open as if ready to say something.

"Mr. Phelps said that Graves had information that he would pass on to the insurance attorneys that would cost him many thousands of dollars and that we would need that money in San Francisco. He wanted to hire someone, and I said I would do it."

"So he was planning on taking you to San Francisco?"

"He said," she laughed. "I knew what I was going to do. And I did it. I knew I would be able to get that insurance money as well. He is so naive. I don't need him or any man, ever again. I am Mrs. Castelleno and I own one of the richest mines in Nevada."

CHAPTER THIRTY-TWO

"WHAT DID Bayliss say when you showed him this report on your interview?" Sheriff Ed Connor was behind his desk reading what Corcoran offered the judge. "This confession puts a wrap on the entire conglomeration of killings and burnings, Corcoran. Damn."

"Packett will be here Monday and is bringing another lawyer with him to represent Rosita. Phelps will have to find one for himself. He's still going to be charged with conspiracy to have Ed Graves murdered and for attempting to withhold evidence."

Corcoran was pacing around the office. "There's something bothering you, Terrence." Connor brought the flask out and poured for the both of them. "What is it?"

"Her complete change, sheriff. From the most dangerous woman I've ever encountered to this meek little child sitting in her jail cell crying, to this authoritative land-and-mine owner who rules her world."

Corcoran shook his head and took a long drink from the tin cup. "Who will we be dealing with when Bayliss calls for a hearing? Which of the many Rosita Chavezes will we have to bring to court?"

"Best bet, my friend, is to plan on having to deal with the worst of them," Connor said. "I'm calling it a day."

Corcoran made his way to the Bonanza Club, his mind filled with questions. *Was it her terrible young life that brought all this on or just simple greed, which every lawman has had to deal with in so many crimes? The lust for wealth is at the bottom of so many crimes but this goes so much deeper than that. I hope that Bayliss shows compassion here and sends her to the home for mental cases.*

Cindy Cook intercepted him as he made his way through the evening crowd toward the bar. "The judge is in the restaurant, Terrence. He wants you to join him. Art Bellows is already there. He's a devil," she giggled, dancing off toward the kitchen.

"Evening, judge. Art. Looks like this spring weather has half the town out."

"Sit down, Corcoran," Bayliss said, rather curtly. "Mr. Bellows and I have been discussing the set of cases you've been working on. Rosita Chavez isn't really the enigma you seem to think. Simply mentally cracked. Loony is a good word for it." He had a platter of pork chops covered in a rich gravy in front of him, a platter designed for a table for four.

"I've never sent anyone to the other side for being crazy and don't want to start now. She realizes that what she's done is wrong?" he asked.

"I didn't get that impression at all, judge. She realizes what she's done, yes, but does she think it was wrong? No. I think she sees herself as doing something that needed to be done. She saw Maria as doing wrong to her marriage but doesn't see herself doing wrong having relations with Maria's husband."

"And these lustful men? How do they fit in?" Bayliss forked another pork chop onto his plate. "Hatfield and Phelps were both enjoying the pleasures of Mrs. Castelleno while Mr. Castelleno was pleasuring Rosita? Is that right?"

"On the money," Corcoran said. "Each seemed to have their own reasons. Hatfield wanted Castelleno's mine. Phelps just wanted pleasure. The old man, too, wanted pleasure but may have seen his shenanigans with Rosita as payback for his wife's infidelity."

"The sheriff showed me the marriage certificate that Chavez wrote up. Worthless. You've done a good job, Corcoran. You too, Bellows. Packett came in on this evening's train so we can wrap this up fast tomorrow morning. How many people have died since this all started? Well, I have no use for gold. I'll settle for a full table served by a wench as full of it as your friend, Cindy Cook. Will you two join me for pie and brandy?"

———

THE MORNING EXPLODED into brilliant spring with not a cloud in sight as Corcoran nudged little Cindy awake. "Gotta get things moving, little girl. The judge said he wanted a big breakfast before he holds court."

"My cupboards are bare, Terrence. I've never seen anyone who can eat that much and still move about. Mr. Henderson sent George Florencio out for more meat.

Told him he wanted two elk and three deer." She laughed trying to get untangled from sheets and blankets. "Are you having breakfast with him?"

"No. Lots to do to get ready for this hearing. Not looking forward to moving Rosita up to the courtroom. I might need some doctoring when this is all over."

"I'll doctor you, Terrence. Oh my, will I doctor you." Corcoran patted her cute little bottom and headed for the sheriff's office. He was humming quietly the whole way.

"Corcoran, you and Lou Foster are the strongest, and Bellows you're right with them. We need to get Chavez out of that cell, up those stairs, and into the courtroom without creating pandemonium. Ideas?"

"Gentleness, sheriff. She responded to gentle talking. I'd like to think it might work again," Corcoran said. He looked to Bellows.

"It did seem to keep her calm. I think if we all show up she'll get defensive and we'll have bedlam all over again. That damn staircase is narrow, solid rock, and if she explodes there, someone is going to get hurt."

"She'll have to have her wrists and ankles manacled," Foster said. "She's so strong she could hurt someone bad on that staircase. Be like dragging a calf to the fire."

The thought, seeing three deputies as buckaroos dragging a calf, Rosita, to be branded, that is to the judge, brought a lot of laughter to the bunch, easing tensions quickly. Dark humor will do that.

"So be it," Ed Connor finally said. "Court's in half an hour. Packett is with Rosita now, so we'd best get moving."

———————

STANLEY PACKETT WAS WIRE THIN, tall, and nearing fifty years on this old world. He'd seen it all. Murderers, thieves, conspiracy nuts, confidence games by the gross in his years as an attorney. He's defended men who kill just for the thrill of it, women who wield their wiles to get the gold, and even children being used for illicit gain. This one was different, and he did not want any part of it.

Why was he here in Eureka County? District Judge Eric Bayliss threatened his license, that's why, and Packett arrived in Eureka late at night. He was looking into the sad yet angry eyes of Rosita Chavez that early morning.

He was standing back several feet from the bars after a quick discussion with jailer Tommy Reilly. He could see the strength in the woman's shoulders and arms and wasn't about to get caught up in them. "I'm the prosecuting attorney, Miss Chavez. Stan Packett. Do you understand the charges that have been filed?"

She gave the slightest shrug, flashed angry and dark eyes at the man but didn't say a word. She was sitting on the edge of the cot glaring at the man. Packett had seen this many times in those who knew they were destined for the hangman's noose. "The charges carry a stiff penalty but if you work your attorney, who will be here shortly, we might be able to save your life. Will you help?"

He started to take a step forward, caught himself, but it was too late. As a cat might strike, Rosita flashed across the cell, reached out and grabbed the skinny and lightweight Packett by his coat. She jerked him up against the bars, wrenching his shoulder between two of them, and grabbed for his neck.

Tommy Reilly, old and half crippled from army service in the Indian wars, from too many years in the saddle wrestling calves and younger buckaroos, wasn't fast, but got his old Colt Walker out and blew Rosita's head almost off her shoulders, splattering the half-unconscious attorney with blood and brains.

Packett was trapped between the bars, Rosita's dead weight keeping him pinned to them, and was slowly suffocating before Reilly could get him free. He slumped to the floor, gasping for breath, fighting to get away from the horrible scene. Reilly was having a hard time trying to pull him from the pool of blood when several people from up in the courthouse descended on them.

"Get Corcoran," Reilly said to the first one down. "Don't nobody touch nothing," he said, "until the sheriff and Corcoran get here. Now, get out, all of you. The woman can't be helped and the man ain't hurt. Go on back to work."

Corcoran, Bellows, Sheriff Connor, and Lou Foster were preparing to make the climb to the courthouse when they heard the single, muffled gunshot. "Trouble," Corcoran said, making for the door. He was halfway up the hill when a man came running down, yelling for him.

"Reilly shot the woman," he yelled and Corcoran raced for the massive stone structure. He had to fight his way through the crowd and down the rock steps to the old jail.

"Oh no," he almost whispered, seeing Packett covered

in blood, and Rosita Chavez's body splayed out in the cell. Reilly was sitting in his chair holding his head, rocking slowly back and forth.

"I had to do it, Terrence. She was choking him to death. Damn fool didn't hear a word I said about not getting close to her. Walked right up to the cell bars. He's all right. That's her blood, not his, but he is lucky I can still make a good shot when I have to." He was trembling from the effort, from the surge of excitement, and from old age.

It was just moments and the rest of the Eureka County sheriff's office arrived, filling the small jail space. Corcoran was standing next to Packett but looking toward Rosita. "Might not be the right thing to say, but I think this is the best way for this to end. She was looking at years in the crazy farm. At her death she was sure she owned the Castelleno mines, was rich beyond thought, and had done right by her strange sense of morals."

Ed Connor told Lou Foster to track down the judge and tell him what happened and then get Doc Whidby. "I need everything in writing, Mr. Reilly. The judge could very well go into fits of anger. Go back to the office and get started. You did the only thing you could do. You saved Mr. Packett's life, Tom. Remember that."

CHAPTER THIRTY-THREE

"The sheriff told me what you said, Corcoran," Judge Bayliss said. They were sitting at a table at the Bonanza Club. "I think I have to agree with you. Rosita Chavez was insane, probably driven that way by the way she was treated in her younger years. Because of your good work her days of killing people were over."

"Of all of them, Bill Phelps is the only one left to face you, judge. Hatfield murdered men, Rosita murdered men, Wellington murdered a man, and Phelps was involved all the way around. Has he approached you?"

"No, he called Packett in and said that he would offer a guilty plea when we hold court tomorrow morning. Actually, I have two cases to hear. Doctor Whidby is asking to be in legal custody of Pedro Castelleno until he reaches adulthood. He and the boy have become very close in these last few weeks."

Bayliss had a smile on his face and watched Cindy Cook come out from the kitchen holding a platter of elk steaks. "Ah, my favorite kitchen wench has brought me a snack. A lovely girl, Corcoran. A woman who can cook as if for a king, has a wild and friendly sense of humor, and is quite good-looking to boot, shouldn't be let to roam about."

He roared with laughter at his comments, slapped Corcoran across the shoulders, and continued. "She needs to be roped and dragged to the fire, Corcoran. You need to put your brand to her, my boy. She's prime or I don't know my women."

Terrence Corcoran reddened, ducked his head, and coughed softly as Cindy put the platter down in front of Eric Bayliss. "He's right you know," she said, jumping in the big man's lap. "You know you need me, Terrence. I sure do need you."

"I think it might be best if we discuss this later tonight. At your place. When the lamp is shut off," he said. He patted her cute little bottom and knew that he would never get married. *The judge is right about Cindy. Any other man would be a fool not to grab her up and rope her tight, but not this old bird. I had my chance with Crazy Hair. Besides, I'm married to this old, bent, and scarred tin badge. And, I'm not through rambling around.*

A LOOK AT BOOK TEN:

To Kill or Not to Kill

WESTERN ACTION, OMINOUS STORMS, AND A FIGHT TO THE DEATH.

In the rugged terrain of Eureka County, where the promise of gold lures dreamers and opportunists alike, Chief Deputy Sheriff Terrence Corcoran finds himself entangled in a web of deception that stretches far beyond the confines of the Eureka Mine and Mill.

When a complex scheme to defraud the mine unravels, leaving the chief assayer brutally murdered, Corcoran's investigation thrusts him into a perilous game where every step forward could be his last. As the tendrils of corruption infiltrate the very heart of the community, false leads run rampant, and Corcoran must navigate a treacherous landscape where the line between ally and adversary blurs.

But in a town where trust is a scarce commodity, how can this every-man lawman pursue justice—while also protecting those whose lives are being threatened?

AVAILABLE NOW

ABOUT THE AUTHOR

Reno, Nevada novelist, **Johnny Gunn**, is retired from a long career in journalism. He has worked in print, broadcast, and Internet, including a stint as publisher and editor of the Virginia City Legend. These days, Gunn spends most of his time writing novel length fiction, concentrating on the western genre. Or, you can find him down by the Truckee River with a fly rod in hand.

"it's been a wonderful life. I was born in Santa Cruz, California, on the north shore of fabled Monterey Bay. When I was fourteen, that would have been 1953, we moved to Guam and I went through my high school years living in a tropical paradise. I learned to scuba dive from a WWII Navy Frogman, learned to fly from a WWII combat pilot (by dad), but I knew how to fish long before I moved to Guam.

"I spent time on the Island of Truk, which during WWII was a huge Japanese naval base, and dived in the lagoon. Massive U.S. air strikes sunk thousands of tons of Japanese naval craft, and it was more than exciting to dive on those wrecks. In the Palau Islands, near Koror, I also dived on Japanese aircraft that had been shot down into the lagoons.

www.ingramcontent.com/pod-product-compliance
Lightning Source LLC
Chambersburg PA
CBHW011027260626
47153CB00020B/2963